A Ruined Wife

*The seductions,
submissions, and
sexual encounters
of ordinary housewives*

Andrea's Story
Part I

Reluctant Tramp

by **Mrs. Jennifer Nite**

FOR ADULTS ONLY

About This Edition

This is a revised edition of the wildly popular eBook available on Kindle. You may ask if the revisions are worth purchasing the paperback. Good question.

The front and back cover photos have changed. (Yes, boys, the lady is a married friend of mine). There are also many grammatical fixes. Finally, there are substantive changes throughout the book which provide more detail in certain areas of the story. Parts II and III in particular have much more detail. The chapters have also been revised, for a total of 40 chapters through the end of Part III. All told, the three parts total well over 500 pages.

That all being said, I usually use eBooks on my iPhone just to pass tedious down time, such as when I'm trapped in an airport waiting hours for a flight. Personally, I am the kind of person who has to own a copy of a book if it's in print. There is just nothing like holding a hard copy of a book in your hands. It also makes it easier for your spouse to innocently "find" the story lying around the house!

– Jennifer

Introduction

The ordinary.

That's the life of most people. We get up in the morning, we go through the work day waiting for it to end, and we come home to take care of our children and husbands. And then we go to bed, roll over, and ... it starts all over again. Day after day. Year after year. The drudgery of married life. I know . . . I've experienced it myself for 16 years.

But sex is not ordinary. Sex is extraordinary. But inevitably sex leaves the marriage after a period of years. And what do you do then? Suffer through life?

This is a series that explores that question from the perspective of several married women, with loving husbands and often with young children. Some are younger ladies, and some are older.

The results are the same -- a sexual awakening that changes their lives. They become ruined to the ordinary sexually-empty drudgery of the monogamous marriage. And their husbands become accepting and often participating cuckolds (archaically known as wittols).

Is it a moral issue? I can't answer that question. It used to be that sexual awareness was a topic explored by men, and often (but not always) shunned by women.

The men's stag films and the pulp fiction novels of the 50s and 60s changed dramatically with the advent of the Internet. Morals widened, sexual freedom has expanded, and pornography is secretly available to everyone virtually for free. And women are now active consumers. MILF is now a universally known word. Being seen as a beautiful MILF is remarkably the goal of many wives and mothers throughout the United States and, indeed, the world.

The transformation of our society is what led to these stories. I do not pass judgment on these ladies or their husbands. I understand what a little on the side can do for one's outlook on life.

The stories speak almost exclusively of the sexual encounters of ordinary housewives and mothers, women I would consider to be genuine ladies. These are the women who are your next-door neighbor, the gorgeous wife you see at the PTO meeting, that tremendously hot girl you see at the office every day.

The places in these stories are everywhere, from their homes to their offices and everywhere in between.

Be warned! The tales of these married women are not for the lighthearted. Unlike most books in this genre, these books are not romance novels and they are not stories of lovemaking.

They are likewise not a collection of short stories that you have to read 10 pages to get to what you want, just to find that it's little or nothing. These are hard core, very explicit stories that get right to the point in great detail. They are XXX, no question about it. The wives present in graphic detail and usually from their perspective the circumstances that led to their seduction . . . blow by blow, so to speak.

It's mainstream encounters, from the single seduction -- often forced for the first time – to threesomes and even the occasional gang action. Their partners are white, black, and everyone else. But there are no water sports, no bondage, no whips and chains, no beating of people, no animals, no children, no incest, and no weird sexual acts. If you need any of that sort of thing, then you will need to go elsewhere.

You should also avoid these books if you are easily offended by filthy, sordid talk, because that is the essence of the seductions. So be careful! These books are so hot you'll burn yourself.

A word of warning before you continue. We won't patronize you, because we trust that you are all mature, consenting adults. But we caution you to seriously consider the ramifications before embarking on the lifestyle presented in this series. Provocative Publishers believes in the importance and value of family relationships.

Jealously and insecurity are the scourge of families. If you are considering an open-marriage kind of lifestyle, please do everything possible to preserve your family. You have a choice. Some people, like we will see with Andrea, didn't have a choice. The exhilaration of the lifestyle was forced upon her, after which she couldn't turn back!

So, if you want to hear the details of the seductions of beautiful housewives and the endless sex they have come to need -- how each has become ruined to the ordinary drudgery of married life -- then read on. You will not be disappointed with these tales of infidelity!

We invite you to read the whole series. They each tell a different story from a different perspective!

Who knows. Maybe some film producer would like to adapt these stories to the screen. There certainly aren't any good XXX films out there that present these kinds of stories versus all of that mindless stupid porn in the world. If you're an interested adult film producer, please give us a shout.

That all being said, let's start with my friend Andrea's story. Well, her three stories!

Chapter One

My name is Andrea, and this my story of how some studs ruined or, perhaps, saved me.

It's a little more than innocence lost. While I now have gaping holes that my husband thinks is like fucking an oil barrel, the bastards also turned me into a cock-crazed size-queen ass slut who just can't live without a load of hot cum running down my throat or being splashed across my face. Let me tell you who I am and how it all started.

I'm 35 years old, and I'm a housewife and mother. My hair is a silky black. I like my hair dresser to alternate between a curled and a wavy look as the mood strikes me.

I have small pouty lips and I always wear red lipstick to match my red nail polish. They're my trademark.

What is my body like, you may be asking. Well, I've always thought that appearance is important because of my job.

I don't hang out in the sun, so my skin has remained clear and smooth. I have a very fair complexion and great legs -- my husband always told me I could be a model.

I would say that I have a shapely body, and I do like to keep in shape. You could call me petite. It's hard to tell that I had a child 8 years ago.

My bra size is 36C, fairly good sized breasts. In fact, my breasts have always been my yardstick of how my body was holding up with age. I am proud that they remain firm and don't sag. I have large, puffy areola that really stand out in a mirror, curving slightly upward and holding rather large nipples. My breasts are definitely the best part of my body after my legs.

I noticed men would look at my legs and breasts quite a bit, but it never bothered me. I took it as a compliment. Hmmm . . . I have to admit that I didn't care for the fathers at school meetings glaring at me, or the men at church looking me over every weekend, because that was immoral, right?

My husband's name is Mark. We've been married for 10 years, and we have a beautiful 8-year old girl named Ginger.

Mark and I were an item in high school, and we got married shortly after Mark and I finished our college programs. He is the only man I've ever been with until I was forcefully seduced. He's calls me an elegant woman, and I call him a very handsome man.

Mark and I had what I thought was an ok sex life up until this incident occurred, but it was boring. Same old missionary sex, and only once a month at that. I loved to get laid, but the same old routine was a bit much. You know what they say, you can't control hormones. And I have more than he does.

Mark likes me to suck him, but I was never much into oral sex. I never could get into it. And I would never let Mark cum in my mouth, because I thought it too disgusting. I certainly wouldn't let him near my ass either. My ass was strictly off limits. Every time he would get close to it, even accidentally, I would yell out that he was in the wrong place.

Yes, I have to admit it. I was a stuck-up bitch when it came to sex. Little did I realize that our marriage was actually miserable because of it, even though I truly loved Mark so much.

It was only last month that I found out the truth about sex.

So much for bad attitudes.

Chapter Two

I work as the assistant manager of a large bank, a professional woman if you will. I am expected to dress professionally every day to go to work. This day was no different.

After my shower, I did my hair as usual. I like to wear it down, over my shoulders. My long fingernails were freshly manicured in red the day before. Matching gloss lipstick, dark eye shadow and mascara, and some perfume finished the makeup.

As normal, I put on a bra and pantyhose. No panties though -- they're just too much with pantyhose in the summer.

Next the clothes.

Today I decided on a skirt and blouse. The skirt was little short and above my knee, I must admit, but not slutty. The blouse was white, and buttoned in the front. It wasn't low cut, but I do leave the top buttons undone.

I then slipped into some high heels, today a pair that strapped at the ankle.

For jewelry, some earrings, a single strand of pearls at the neck, and an ankle bracelet. Finally, my wedding rings -- a gold band and a ½-carat solitaire.

I was ready for work -- what I thought would be another uneventful day.

I've been at my job for 5 years, and I thought thinks were going well until that day. I went into a meeting with my asshole boss Jack and some other bank people.

The meeting was to discuss an error I had made. Jack screamed at me, as usual. He called me a fuck up and told me how stupid I was. He really took me down a few notches, ending the meeting by telling me to get out of his sight.

I was fed up, too, so I took an early lunch at 10:00 in the morning, depressed as all hell. I hated my job.

Mark and Ginger were out of town visiting his parents, so I didn't want to bother him with a phone call. I decided I would deal with this myself.

I drove around trying to calm down, but I got more depressed. I didn't know what to do to.

As I drove around, I passed a small country and western bar that had a truck stop next to it, the Roundup.

I normally didn't drink all that much, maybe a bottle of beer a month, and I never go to bar rooms. What the hell, I thought. A lunch-time drink.

So I stopped and went on in.

There weren't too many people in the place since it had just opened. I went to the bar, ordered a beer, and sat at a table in the corner. I just sipped on the beer thinking about what had just happened at work. It was then that I met Bill.

I had been drinking about an hour when this trucker came in. In no time he came over to my table and just sat down.

Bill said I looked depressed, and he told me to cheer up. That obvious!

At first I was a little apprehensive about talking to this stranger, but given the beer it was no time before I was relaxed enough to tell this stranger my problems!

Bill told me he was a trucker. He said he spends the night in his rig at truck stops, and this time he was at the one next to the bar.

Bill was an older man, he told me he was 52. He was a little taller than me and not at all a bad looking guy, but he had a good sized gut and only wore a tee-shirt. He was obviously the rough type, as he had tattoos all over his muscled arms. But he seemed nice, and was very polite.

Bill kept a good conversation going, helping to be feel better about my miserable day. Bill asked me all about myself. I told him about my husband, my job, and the bad day I was having.

Bill did his best to cheer me up, complimenting me on how nice I looked. He even moved his chair closer to mine, and put his hands on my shoulder when I told him how my boss treated me so bad.

Being a little tipsy from the beers, I didn't noticed when my skirt rode up, giving Bill a great view of my legs the whole time. I should have figured out then what was coming, especially given the way Bill kept leering at my legs and cleavage. I didn't really care. What could it hurt?

At that moment in my life, I needed those compliments. And I was enjoying the attention he was giving me. Here I was, a middle-aged married woman and mother. What woman wouldn't feel good about the attention. Who cares if he looked me over?

Yes, I liked the attention. I guess as a kind of reward, I made a point of freshening my lipstick and perfume when I went to the ladies room.

Bill and I talked more about work. He told me more about what he did, and he told me about all of the interesting places he had been to.

Bill jumped at my questions about his truck, and invited me to come see his rig. I had never seen an 18-wheeler up close, so I agreed. I always found them kind of mysterious, a giant unknown that races past you on the freeway.

The beers must have been talking, because I didn't anticipate what was coming next.

Chapter Three

When we got to the truck, Bill showed me the cab and let me sit in the driver's seat. He boosted me up, help me by putting his big hands on my waist to lift me up.

When I got down, he opened the sleeping compartment and told me that was where he had to live on the road. He took me by my waist and helped me up again. I didn't think anything of it.

As I crawled in, I felt my skirt catch on the door. I didn't give it a second though when I rode up a bit.

The sleeper was small, pretty much just a bed that you could only kneel up when inside of it. There was a small light turned on in the corner.

Bill jumped up behind me and shut the door.

We talked for a few minutes about what it was like to live on the road in such a cramped space. There wasn't much one could do in here, I thought.

I turned to get out, but I was bush-wacked, so to speak. When I reached for the door handle, Bill came up behind me and wrapped his arm around my waist. He was fast.

Bill immediately started running his free hand between my legs and up my skirt, and started kissing my neck.

"You're a pretty woman, Andrea," he said calmly.

I thanked him, and reached for the door handle. As I did so, he wrapped his arms around me and ran his hand down my arm.

Bill reached down for my hand as it was on the handle and took hold of it. He pulled me around, and I found myself a few inches from his face.

He wrapped his arms around me tighter and pulled me close to him. He started to rub my ass as he spoke to me, his growing hard-on becoming more and more apparent to me.

"I love a beautiful woman Andrea, and you're so sweet," he said. He then ran his hand under my skirt, squeezing my ass check. He leaned forward to kiss me.

I pulled back and tried to break away. He just held me tighter.

"I want you, Andrea," he said, "I really want to make it with you," he boldly said.

I was horrified.

I tried to pull away, but he pushed me back against the door until I couldn't move, and pushed his lips against mine.

I couldn't believe that this man old enough to be my father was doing this. But I didn't want to anger him, so I turned my head and gave him a light kiss on the cheek. I then told him I had to go.

He asked me to stay a bit.

"Bill, you're a wonderful man and I really appreciate how much you like me," I said, "but I'm happily married. I can't do this."

Bill wouldn't hear of it. His attitude became more forceful.

"Goddamn, Andrea, he doesn't appreciate you. Look how fucking miserable your life is! A little fun won't hurt."

I had to admit to myself that he was right about my miserable life, due in no small part to a dull sex life. But this was wrong.

Bill just pushed me up against the door again and kissed me again. By now I could feel his raging hard-on pushing against me. I struggled, but it did no good.

Bill forced his tongue between my lips and into my mouth. His tongue worked furiously to dart around my lifeless tongue.

Bill then reached around me with his under my skirt, pushing his hand against my pussy. I could feel that I was starting to get wet, and his fingers felt great rubbing my clit.

"I think a good fuck is what you need Andrea," he said as he reached around and pulled my pussy tight against his hard on.

I was disgusted. I didn't know what to say to the bastard. I told him again that I wanted to leave. But he didn't stop.

He ran his hand up my skirt and literally pushed his finger through my pantyhose. He then pulled up, tearing a large hole in the crotch of my pantyhose to reveal my pussy.

My hairy pussy was dry, but a sensation came over me when the cool air blew over my cunt lips.

Bill started running his fingers through over bush and into my pussy, saying crude things as he stroked my cunt lips with his rough hands.

"What you need is a big hard cock right here," he told me.

I tried to resist, but he pulled me tighter to him. I could feel his swelling hard-on grinding into my pussy.

Bill kissed me again, forcing my mouth open to take his tongue. I didn't respond. I didn't want to entice him.

"Such a sweet face!" he told me, "I think it needs a wad blown on it!"

Oh my God, I thought!

I told him Bill again that I was married and wanted to leave.

Upon hearing the words, Bill spun me around an threw me onto the bed. I landed flat on my back in the middle of the small bed, the force of the landing caused my skirt to rise up close to my waist.

Bill jumped down on the bed before me, and forced my legs apart with his strong hands. In an instant he dived for my cunt and started was licking me through the gash in the pantyhose.

I resisted and squirmed, but I quickly realized as his tongue worked its way through my twat that I was in heaven! In no time my labia was inflame as Bill spread my cuntal lips with his fingers and worked his tongue around them. He fingered my pussy as he licked my clitoris.

My God! My husband never made me feel that way. Despite my struggling, I soon had the first of the many torrential orgasms I would have that day.

Bill kept licking away for about 10 minutes, giving me a second powerful orgasm that caused me to thrust my hips in the air.

The bastard was driving me insane with lust. I was reveling in the passionate sensations stirring between my legs.

Bill then stopped, sensing that I was ready to be mounted.

Bill stopped sucking on my clit and looked up at me. He looked at me straight in the eye as he firmly cupped my bush with his large hand.

"Damn!" he said, "I can't wait to feel this tight pussy squeezing the cum out of my cock!"

Bill started to pull himself up. I glanced down and saw Bill him reach for his belt. When he was straight up before me, he started to unstrap his belt. Bill looked adamant that he was going to fuck me then and there.

My head was spinning. Oh my God! I couldn't let this brute fuck me, as good as his pussy licking felt. I was a married woman, a mother, and he was a total stranger. I didn't want another man to have me.

There was also the pregnancy thing. I wasn't using any birth control. My husband and I have sex to seldom, we just use the rhythm method. I didn't know if this was an ok day or not, because we never had sex! For all I knew, I was ovulating. I didn't relish the idea of having to get an abortion because I started the day depressed!

I also wondered if this guy had HIV. How often did he do this kind of thing? And with what kind of women? Little did I realize at the time that I was about to become a bareback queen.

My mind was racing to find a way out of the predicament I found myself in, but my body was literally on fire from Bill's incredible cunt licking. As much as my mind wanted to end it, my body didn't share my concern!

Unfortunately the beer started to talk. It gave me bad advice. It told me to appease him.

A sense of urgency overtook me. I had to keep this bastard from studding me. There was no doubt about it, this was not the time to get seduced.

I was ready to do whatever it took to avoid it. In my drunken state, I thought if I could just get Bill to cum like he did to me, he would be spent and that would be the end of it. At least it would keep him from taking what he wanted, or so I thought at the time.

Just give him a blowjob I thought, not realizing that I would be assisting him in seducing my innocent virtue away from me.

I looked down at Bill and told him not yet. He asked what I meant, and I told him I should probably return the service he just gave me. I put my hands on his shoulders and pulled Bill up to me, finally returning his kiss. Bill kissed me back, fondling my ass under my skirt as he did so.

After he kissed me, Bill looked down at me with wide grin.

"So, you want to taste my cock?" he asked with a wide lecherous grin.

I just looked up at him, not knowing what to say. Bill knew what he wanted me to say, and he asked me again.

"Do you want to suck my cock?"

I couldn't believe what I said. Almost instinctively, I said yes. I wanted to get this over with.

Bill rolled off from me and gestured for me to go down to the bulge between his legs as he unzipped his pants.

I obeyed, pulling myself around until I was on my knees in front of him. I reached in and felt his swelling prick inside his underwear.

Bill told me to take his pants down, gloating over his victory.

I reached up and unbuttoned his pants. I tugged the trousers down to his knees. Bill pulled his legs out and they were off.

The bulge of his hard-on was now fully visible in his underwear. I couldn't believe how big the bulge was.

Bill told me to keep going, so I reached up to his waist and yanked down his underwear.

Bill had a massive hard-on. His stiff cock just sprang out, slapping me on the face.

Once that hard cock was out, I was stunned. The fucking thing was stuck out like a board, hard and throbbing for a married woman.

Bill's old prick was bigger than my husband's. My husband had a decent cock, I thought, but it wasn't that thick. Bill's cock had to be 10" long and was exceptionally thick. It had a massive, bulbous head to it that was perfectly mushroomed shaped.

Bill was ready. The veins on his cock were engorged with blood, and rose out of the hard rubbery flesh. This wasn't going to be like a night of making love with my husband, I thought. This was raw animalistic sex, Bill's massive cock throbbing like an horny monster waiting to attack.

I really thought that I had done the right thing. His prick was way too enormous to fuck. I knew I couldn't take that massive prick between my legs. Besides, he would stretch the shit out of me if he got this slab of meat in me. How would I explain that to my husband, a man with a thin 6" cock?

I admit that I was intrigued by this big cock waiving in front of my face, and something in me wanted so much to touch it. Besides, I have to.

There was no doubt about it. Sucking this animal off was a small price to pay to keep Bill's monster prick and his seed out of my pussy. I knew what I had to do.

While I was certainly no expert at oral sex, I knew I had to get this bastard off in my mouth. I somehow had to. While I never let my husband cum in my mouth, I knew I had no choice but to let Bill be the first.

I went to go and touch the cock, and Bill put his hands around my head. He pulled my head closer to his cock, and then he suddenly pulled back as I was about to take it into my mouth.

Bill stopped me, grabbing his dick himself. He then introduced me to his prick by rubbing the massive cock head and shaft over my cheeks and across my chin. The whole scene was so lewd and decadent. That fiery hot prick burned into me.

I kept turning my head, trying to get the shaft into my mouth so I could do my job. Bill wouldn't let me, teasing me instead. He must have thought I was a woman on a mission to suck his cock.

When Bill finally brought the cock head to my lips, he easily pushed it into my opening mouth. I pushed my tongue to swirl it around the head. I gently sucked on the head, already starting to feel the pre-cum oozing from the prick. I felt nervous having this stranger's big cock in my mouth.

It's one thing to have oral sex with your husband. This was a completely different experience. I was having what I could not have. I was doing what my religion forbid. It was a surreal, exciting experience.

Yes, I was forced to submit to a horny brute, but I must admit in retrospect that I secretly enjoyed what was happening! I felt like an adulteress, a common tramp being used by a stud to service his sexual needs. But I was in a predicament. I had no time to worry about morals now. I had to avoid getting screwed by this man.

I continued to run my tongue around the mushroom head, sucking it very carefully. The sensation of the smooth head was incredible! I still couldn't believe that I was letting myself be used by this stranger to service his magnificent cock! And I couldn't believe my body was enjoying it!

Slowly, I pushed the massive cock deeper and deeper into my mouth. I couldn't help but enjoy the feeling of having Bill's tool in my mouth. I reached up and started to stroke the cock as I sucked, feeling that hard rod in my soft hand..

I started to gently give Bill a hand job as I sucked him. I squeezed the base of his cock, and his cock swelled from the blood. That cock head increased in size significantly. I sucked on it again as it remained puffed up.

Bill pulled his cock away again, teasing me. He grabbed his cock hard, causing to swell again. He slapped the swollen giant cockhead on my open lips. It was as hard and smooth as glass. The pre-cum from the cock head stuck to my lips, creating a long string stuck to my red lips as he pulled the dick up. It was a truly decadent scene.

"You really want this big cock in your mouth, don't you Andrea?"

My husband never talked to me like that! I felt like such a harlot, so sexual and desirable. Oh yes, Bill's words struck a chord in my body. I never realized how sensual such filthy talk could be. I found myself welcoming what he said.

I said yes to Bill's question. The incredible whorish feeling Bill and his language created in me was overwhelming. But I knew that the sooner I could finish this task the better.

Bill brought the hot cock back to my cheek, and I turned my head to service him.

"You love to suck cock, don't you, you little slut?"

The bastard obviously liked degrading his fucks, but the vulgar language further stirred the slutty depths of my soul. It was a new experience for me hearing his kind of language, and I found it exhilarating. The more he said, the more I found myself wanting him to talk that way to me.

I wanted to drive this man so crazy that he would shoot his load and be done with me. So I teased him back with the language he loved to inflame his passion.

"Oh yes," I said as I slowly licked my lips, "I love to suck big cocks!"

Oh my God! What was I saying? But I couldn't stop. Not yet. I had a job to finish.

With that, Bill brought his cock up to my lips again like he was rewarding me. I darted my tongue out, flicking it over the head with a fast pace.

Bill then started to get really nasty.

"How bad do you want to suck my big cock, you horny bitch?"

I decided to give him a show. I reached out and grabbed the throbbing shaft dangling over my face, stroking it hard up and down the entire length of the shaft with my soft hands.

I was shocked that I could barely wrap my hand around Bill's cock.

As I jerked off the cock, I looked at him straight in the eye and softly told him what he wanted to hear.

"Please let me suck your big cock, Bill, please."

Getting excited by how he was talking to me and treating me, I didn't wait for his answer. I took Bill's hot prick in my hand, my lips snapping shut on the cock head of the enormous fuck stick.

I forced my mouth open further and shoved it in my mouth as far as I could. I started to furiously suck the cock, pushing it in and out of my mouth as fast as I could.

The whole time I kept my hand on the shaft, holding it tight and jerking it up and down. I wanted to make this bastard cum as fast as I could.

When I was sucking on his pecker, Bill reached down and squeezed one of my tits through my bra. Not wanting to anger him while I worked on my task, I didn't stop him as he copped a feel of my tits.

Bill then pushed his hand into my bra and cupped my breast. The feeling of this strangers rough hands stroking my breast was foreign to me, but exciting at the same time.

"Oh, sweetheart, you have nice firm tits!" he said as he popped one tit out of my bra.

Bill then proceeded to unbutton my blouse. It took no time for my blouse to fall totally open from the expert action of Bill's hands. He then popped the other tit out.

There I was, my bra still on, and both tits handing out to be fondled by this old bastard.

"I want to suck those big tits of yours," he then said calmly.

I felt powerless.

Bill had half of my blouse undone in no time, and he popped my tits over the top of my bra. Seeing that I had a bra that snapped in front, he popped it open. My tits came loose. My long black hair draped down and covered my nipples. It was quite a sensual feeling as Bill caressed my breasts through my long hair.

I knew I couldn't stop him from suckling my swollen tits, and at that point I couldn't say that I cared that he did. That caressing through my hair was driving me nuts.

It was driving Bill crazy too.

"Damn!" he said, "maybe I'll cum on those hot tits instead!"

The caressing and filthy talk started to arose me. I impulsively unbuttoned the rest of my blouse as I held Bill's throbbing rod in my mouth.

But my mind eventually cleared, and I realized that the new sensations I was enjoying from the attention Bill was giving my tits was not important. I became determined that I would get this man to cum soon. He was welcome to cum on my tits as long he would just cum!

I knew that Bill had to have a tight sensation on his shaft to make him cum. So I pushed the cock into my throat as deep as I could manage. I could feel my face contorting from the sheer size of the bastard's hard prick. I stopped stroking the shaft for a moment and cupped his balls as I forced more and more of it into my mouth. Bill was moaning out loud in no time.

After I was able to work the shaft in good distance more, I started bobbing my head up and down on his cock. My saliva was all over it, making it easier to push the cock head in and out of my small throat.

"Ohhhh, fuck" he said.

Brushing my hair around my tits, Bill started to rub them harder with his rough hands, squeezing each nipple every few seconds. He tweaked and twisted my nipples, making them grow big and hard in no time.

"Damn you have nice tits!" he said as he cupped them, "and those nipples are driving me crazy!"

Bill squeezed my tits more, taking my nipples and twisting them harder and harder. The sensation was overwhelming as he pinched and pulled. My husband never handled my tits in such a rough, sexual manner. I found it incredibly arousing.

"Your fucking husband is one lucky bastard," he said.

He kept rubbing, and I kept bobbing.

Bill went on with the commentary.

"I knew a stiff prick in your mouth would cheer you up."

I moaned in response. There was no denying it. It did cheer me up.

Bill's sordid talk made me a woman in heat. The feeling of that fat dick in my mouth and a stranger's rough hands rubbing my tits was starting to be too much.

I was getting aroused, as Bill found out when my nipples thickened in his fingers. He pulled my nipples out as far as he could.

"You like getting your tits rubbed and squeezed, don't you slut?"

Oh god, did I. It was igniting a hot fire in me, preparing my body for his hard cock.

I licked the shaft all over, and noticed a long string of pre-cum running from the massive cock head to my chin. I moved my head closer, sucking the cum string in like it was food.

Bill reached down and pulled my body sideways in front of him. He then slipped his hand between my legs and started gently rubbing my thighs. He was causing me to moan again from the sensation of his rough hands on my smooth skin. As he rubbed my leg, he occasionally pushed a finger into my slit. He was driving me crazy.

Bill then told me to rub his balls. I reached up with my hand and cupped his hairy balls. As I licked between the shaft and the great cock head, I carefully caressed the bottom of his heavy old sack, first with my fingers and then with my nails.

It was so hairy, and incredibly leathery. His balls had to be as big as golf balls.

"Ohhhh," Bill cried. I found the mark.

"Ohhhh," he moaned again. I was close.

His hands worked harder, moving up to my bush. He fingered me as he moaned.

"Fuck you're wet Andrea," he said.

I moaned again as I started to suck on his balls.

Bill moaned again as I drooled on the massive cock head and licked the ridge of the mushroom. I then sucked his cock deep into my mouth without warning, continuing to rub his balls with my fingernails.

Just when I thought Bill was about to cum, he took his hands and brought them to the sides of my head. He grabbed my head and started forcing his cock deeper into my mouth. I started to gag, and Bill pulled out a little.

Bill told that if I relaxed, he would make me a professional cock sucker. Intrigued by the thought that I could make this man any hornier, I did as he said.

Bill pushed a little more, forcing his throbbing cock into my throat. It was a lot, and I gagged again.

"I'm not going to tell you again, you fucking cunt, relax."

I was sexually charged by what I was doing, but I managed to calm down by the time Bill slowly worked the throbbing snake into down my throat. It was an incredible feeling having that massive cock head lodged firmly in my throat.

Once Bill finally had his cock into my mouth up to his balls, he withdrew. He pushed his cock in again until his balls were resting on my chin. He worked his cock in and out of my throat slowly a few times, remolding my throat to his large cock.

Being a master cocksman, Bill was eventually able to freely mouth fuck me. Intent on fucking my mouth like a cunt, he grabbed the sides of my head and barbarically started a rhythm of pushing his big cock as far into my throat as he could, and then pulling it out until my teeth caught the ridge of his massive cock head.

Bill did this faster and faster, truly training me to deep throat a sizeable cock like a pro. The deep throat training went on for a fair period of time. When Bill suddenly stopped assisting me, he had me hooked.

I instinctively continued deep throating him as he stroked his fingers through my hair, periodically pulling the long fuck stick all the way out to jack it in my face. I was quite satisfied with myself when I pulled his cock out of my throat and noticed a thick string of cum running from his cock head to my lips. I quickly re-impaled myself on the cock, taking the strong of cum with me.

I slowly pushed the rod in to my throat again, savoring the taste of the bastard's sweet cum. I forced my tongue out as my throat was impaled by the cock, barely being able to run it against his musty balls. I could definitely get hooked on this, I thought!

Bill stopped my deep throating of his magnificent cock, saying that he was getting ready to cum. He told me to jerk his cock while I sucked on the head. Doing as I was told, I pushed and pulled on the long shaft faster and harder each time.

"Ohhhh," "Ohhhh,", "Ohhhh, you fucking cunt," Bill cried.

He moaned and moaned, obviously loving the service his big cock was getting.

"Oh God!" he cried, "suck me off!"

I continued servicing his horny the tool. My goal was almost accomplished.

"Oh fuck!" he said, "I'm getting ready to blow my load!"

I thought he was going to blow his load in my mouth. But Bill denied, robbing me of my accomplishment. He reached down and grabbed his cock, telling me to lay back on the bed and to close my eyes. I did as I was ordered by the old cock master.

When I was on my back, Bill straddled my chest and stared to fuck my tits. I could tell the hot prick burn against my flesh.

"Damn, these tits are hot," he said, "squeeze them together."

I pushed my tits together, making a tight tit-cunt for Bill. His hot prick felt so wonderful stroking my tits as Bill reached back and fingered my pussy. He was stroking his cock off between my tits!

"God Andrea," he moaned, "your tight cunt is so wet!"

He then stopped, and I thought for a moment that he was going to mount me. At that moment, I didn't know if I would fight him if he did! But he didn't.

Bill started to jack off the huge cock, stopping only to slap it hard against my face and tits. Bill didn't want to fuck me, I thought! No, he wanted to see his sticky wad on my face.

Suddenly, Bill tensed up and his cock started to blow. He arched back, and the first puddle of cum came splashing down on my cheeks and nose. It was quickly followed by another on my chin that ran down to my pearls, and a third across my lips. Another wad ended up in my hair.

I couldn't believe how much this man was cumming. Bill kept dumping massive chunks of his load all over my face. And the feeling was incredible! My God, his cum was so hot against my skin. I have to say, it truly felt wonderful.

When Bill was finally finished, my face was soaked in cum. I could feel it all over, glossed over my lips and dripping off from my chin! I felt like such a whore!!!

After being trained to suck that massive cock and tasting that first load, the hot cum that was scalding into my skin sent me over the edge. It was like something inside me snapped. It was all so decadent. I loved it!

I never cared for the salty taste of Mark's semen. Something was different this time, however. Maybe it was the taste of the lipstick mixed with the cum, I thought. I don't know. All I know is that I loved it.

I ran my tongue out and ran it around my lips, catching a chunk of cum that was nearby. I wanted to taste more. I brought the wad into my mouth and savored the tantalizing mixture of lipstick and cum.

As I started to get more with my hands, I could feel how silky smooth and creamy it was. It felt so wonderful against my fingers as I licked it off. But Bill grabbed my arm.

"Stop swilling my cum, I want to enjoy what I did to your pretty little face."

Chapter Four

When Bill was done unloading on my face, he laid down next to me, holding the arm that was out to collect more of his cum.

I was exhausted at the suck job I just gave him, and I just wanted to wipe the cum chunks from my face and regain my composure before I left.

When Bill laid next to me, I thought he wanted to gloat over what he had just done to some man's pretty young wife.

But Bill wasn't through with me yet. I would soon find out that he wanted the prize, and that the voluntary blowjob I gave him only solidified my fate. Bill was determined to turn me into a cock-starved whore.

Bill looked in my eyes and started again with the dirty talk – the talk that aroused me so much when I was blowing him. He gently caressed my exposed breasts.

"That had to be the best blowjob I've ever had," he said, "you're quite a cock sucker Andrea."

He leaned over and kissed my sticky lips, and I instinctively kissed him back.

"Did anyone ever tell you how beautiful you look with a load of cum on your face?"

He kissed me again.

"You loved having my big cock in your mouth, didn't you?"

As he kissed me a third time, I had to admit to myself that I really did. I loved taking that big cock down my throat, rubbing his balls, and causing him to explode with such force.

At that point, Bill took my hand and brought it to his cock. Still thinking about what I had done and what it felt like, I couldn't help but rub that massive cock I had just sucked.

We just laid there for a few minutes, Bill puling wads of his cum off from my face and rubbing it into my tits, all the while as I stroked his sticky cock. Ah, the feeling of that cum as he massaged it into my tits!

Bill looked at my face and into my eyes, enjoying the site of the giant wads of cum he left on my face and was spreading across my chest. He took another huge chunk of his cum off from my face and brought the wad down to my pussy.

The old stud started rubbing his hot cum into my bush, mixing it with my own wetness. He cupped my cunt hard, and pushed cum inside of me with his fingers. It was an incredibly exciting feeling.

"You really want me to stroke my prick through your tight little cunt, don't you Andrea?"

I then realized that he was starting to get aroused again. Without thinking, by now I was stroking his massive cock until it was hard again. I guess I brought it on myself, I thought as the cock hardened in my hand.

I couldn't let my prior work be in vain, so I stopped rubbing his cock. But Bill continued to work his wad into my cunt, stroking my lips and clit through the torn pantyhose. It was just too late to deny him.

Despite the risk I was taking with his cum being spread over my cunt lips and pushed into my slit, it felt so damn good.

Bill pressed on.

"You really want to get your cunt screwed by my big prick, don't you Andrea?"

My mind cleared somewhat as I heard his words. I had to stop this from happening. This had to stop now before he did screw me. I pulled my cunt away from his hand and started to get up.

I told Bill that I really had to leave because my husband was waiting for me. Bill obviously didn't believe it, probably remembering that I had told him earlier that Mark was out of town with my daughter.

Bill ignored what I said, leaning over me and pushed me back down.

"I've gotta screw that tight little cunt of yours Andrea," he said coldly.

Bill kissed me again, gripped my pussy harder with his rough hand. The new force of Bill's hand job instinctively caused me to spread my legs.

"You've been looking to get laid by a big hard cock, haven't you Andrea?"

My mind raced. Was I going to be raped by this old bastard? But how could it be rape, I wanted to feel his cock in me so bad?

I didn't have time to decide. Without waiting for a reply, Bill crawled between my legs and proceeded to mount me.

"You shouldn't be such a fucking cock tease Andrea," he said in a slow, relaxed manner.

Bill's legs had forced apart mine, and he reached down with his hand. Bill grabbed his stiff prick and placed the head at the tight hole of my dripping pussy.

I was afraid Bill was going to split me in two with that cock of his, but he gently rubbed the throbbing head over my cunt lips and clit which allowed me to relax.

Pinned as I was, I realized that there was nothing I could do to prevent this horny trucker from laying me. I gave up and succumbed to the fact that I was going to get laid.

Being pinned down by this trucker, I could barely move when he started to push the massive cock head into me. I could feel every inch as the smooth giant head parted my cunt lips. I looked down and saw Bill slowly pushing that rock hard prick into me.

The big cock head was too much. I felt cunt lips open wide as Bill worked his cock into me. My eyes opened wide as my mouth dropped open.

"Aggggh," I cried, clutching the sheets on the bed around me.

Bill pushed harder, getting about a few inches into me.

"God damn it, your pussy is tight Andrea," he said coldly.

While my pussy was moist from all of the excitement, I was still worried his massive cock would split me open.

"You're too big," I cried, as I used my hands to pull my body up and away from his cock.

Like a conquering stud, Bill then reached under my legs with his arms and pushed my legs high, keeping me from moving away from him any further.

I looked down between my spread legs, and I saw Bill's long, thick cock partly lodged between my legs. The sight caused me to gasp a breath of air, and I looked up at Bill.

"Oh God!" I slowly moaned from the sight between my legs.

Bill grinned down at me, so happy that he was bedding a married woman in the cab of his truck. He told me so.

"You're one hot bitch, Andrea, you'll love it," he promised.

I hoped he was right.

Bill pressed on, not about to stop again until he had his fiery big cock firmly imbedded between my legs. He forced his prick up my twat with one long, slow stroke.

Bill was stretching my cunt to accommodate the huge pulsating fuck stick that was being jammed into it. His cock truly felt enormous and filled me completely. The bastard just took me, eventually succeeding in burying his cock deep between my legs.

The deeply imbedded stiff cock caused me to moan again from the bottom of my being in exquisite submission -- it felt as hard as steel. I never thought a man's cock could feel so hard . . . and so damn good.

I could help it. I started to cum on Bill's prick. There was nothing I could do to stop my body from the pleasure Bill's was giving it. I think Bill could tell as I moaned.

"You love it now, eh Andrea?" he said, "you fucking cunt!"

"Go ahead," he added as he started to stroke me, "cum on Bill's big cock."

I did as I was told!

"Oh God!" I groaned, "I'm cumming!"

My sultry comment was Bill's cue to royally fuck me, the bastard beginning to deep hump me with his big old cock. The powerful strokes started with great friction, my ravished cunt having snapped shut on the massive invader.

Bill was a master. He simply yanked the engorged cock out, and pounded it back in, clearly savoring the feeling of my hot, tight cunt. In no time the stud's cock ran completely in and out of me.

He took long, swift strokes, each time mercilessly impaling me with his big cock into me all the way to his balls. With each hard stroke I could feel my insides being stretched open, my cum starting to flow to lubricate the channel for the massive fuck stick.

Bill's pace picked up, and soon the bastard was long dicking me fast and furiously. I could literally see his hairy ass as it raised high into the air, each forceful thrust pounding his great cock deep into my cunt. Deep stroke after deep stroke.

My body betrayed me, and soon I was writhing in delight as the bastard enjoyed me. He promised me I would love it, and he was right. I was in heaven.

As I listened to the sound of Bill's big hairy sack slapping against my ass, I started to cum again and again. An animalistic raw sexuality was awakening within me, and there was nothing I could do to stop it.

"Oh, Oh, Oh," I moaned.

The bastard humped me like a horny dog, and he had me moaning like a whore in no time. He was ripping my cunt open like a stud bull in heat. I knew there was no stopping him until he unloaded his seed inside of me.

Oh God! The feeling of laying there with my skirt hiked and my pantyhose torn, cum chunks still on my face, and this crude old stud briskly stroking my cunt with that huge prick was simply incredible. I can't deny it. I was in total bliss.

My cunt, too, was changing its outlook on life, being remolded by the shape of this Bill's big cock. The more he violently ravished my cunt, the more I realized that I loved being screwed by this man! I would have done anything for him at that point.

My tight cunt snugly formed around his massive cock, which obviously gave Bill wicked pleasure too. He continued with his dirty talk as my orgasms continued.

"Damn did you need a good, hard fucking Andrea," -- something he gave me that day.

Oh God, did I get laid! I knew each time I felt the massive cock head bang home that Bill was giving me the fucking of my life.

Bill's big hot cock was overwhelming. Our bodies were starting to be too hot, sweat beading on our faces. My lust was quickly growing.

Bill had me helping him in no time, the vile talk escaping uncontrollably from me. He was remaking me with his version of sex.

"Give it to me, you fucker. Rape me! RAPE ME! OPEN ME UP WITH THAT BIG COCK, YOU FUCKING HORNY BASTARD."

Bill was happy to oblige. He reached up to put his arms around my head, and I dropped my legs and ground my high heels into the bed. I wrapped my arms around his back and pushed my cunt back as hard as I could to meet every long thrust into my cunt.

Bill and I started kissing as we fucked, our tongues darting in and out of each others mouths. He then stopped and placed his head next to my cum soaked cheek.

I cooed in his ear, "Give me a good hard fucking Bill."

Slowing for a moment, Bill replied as he started licking my ear.

"You fucking slut . . . ohhhh . . . take my hard cock up your tight married cunt!"

He then started thrusting deeper and harder than he ever had before.

"Oh God Bill," I whispered in his ear, "fuck my horny wet cunt!"

The bastard continued to hump me like a crazed madman, making my tits bounce back and forth as he gave it to me. He laid me like I had never been laid before!

After we fucked for what seemed an eternity, I swear I could feel Bill's cock begin to swell and twitch inside my pussy. He was about to cum.

"Oh fuck Andrea, you fucking cunt," he said, "I'm gonna cream between your legs!"

As horny as I was, reality was still a part of my conscience. I tried to stop him.

"Don't cum in me, Bill, I'm not taking birth control."

It was the wrong thing to say. It only excited the bastard more. Bill looked down at me and grinned.

"Oh God, I'm gonna splash those sweet eggs of yours," he moaned.

"No!!!!" I begged.

Bill was merciless as he started to cum inside of me.

"Fuck you . . . cunt!"

Bill slammed the fat prick into me intent on impregnating my fertile womb. His back tensed, and his huge prick injected its hot man seed deep into my cunt. I was surprised he had any left after the blowjob I gave him, but he did have more. I could feel it slop up my cunt.

After what Bill just said and feeling his hot seed being stroked into my cunt walls, I came too. I just couldn't stop my body. I'm sure my pussy was milking the seed deep into my womb.

After Bill came, he slowed his strokes. Finally, he just fell on me, letting his prick soften in my cunt. I could fell his sweaty face against mine.

The passion starting to pass, I thought about my husband. How could I tell him I let some old man with a big cock cream between my legs? The bastard just emptied his balls in my cunt. What did I do to myself? My revelation probably caused this stud to shoot cum from the deepest part of his balls. Did he knock me up and implant me with a bastard child?

As the cum started to seep from my slit and into my torn pantyhose, I knew that Bill thoroughly soaked my ripe eggs with a copious wad of sperm.

Chapter Five

I just laid there, deep in thought.

I got laid! I got laid by a total stranger! And I liked it!!! No, I LOVED IT!!! Bill really gave it to me, and for the first time in my life I felt like a real woman.

Bill rolled off from me, keeping his arm over my waist. I continued to reflect on what I had just done as he caressed me, and how sexy I felt despite the risk I had taken.

I looked at Bill and asked him, "Do you do this often?" He replied with a gloat in his voice.

"Ruin housewives for their husbands?" he asked with a laugh. "Every chance I get!"

That summed it up. Bill broke me in sexually, something my husband was never able to do. Bill also ruined me in the process. I just didn't know it yet.

"You're a great lay, Andrea, I hope you had fun."

I smiled as he went on, asking "So, do I get to have a souvenir?"

He asked what he wanted, and he said he would like to have my pantyhose. They were all torn and cum soaked anyway, so I knew I would never use them again.

When I told Bill he could have them, he reached under his bed. I was shocked when he pulled out a brand new pair of stockings that had a seam running down the back. What a sex maniac, I thought.

"A lady like you should be wearing these anyway," he said. "Go ahead, put them on," he ordered.

What the hell, I though. I unstrapped my high heels and pulled off my pantyhose while Bill got the new stocking out of the package. I slipped the stockings on my legs, pulling them up on my thighs. I put my shoes back on, Bill watching me intently the entire time.

I never wear stockings, but these really made me feel sexy. I don't know why. Maybe just getting laid added to the feeling. It was time to fix my bra, button my blouse and leave.

Bill asked me if I would model his gift first as I got dressed. So I did as he asked, holding up my skirt to reveal my cum-mated wet pussy.

"You're an incredibly beautiful woman," he said, asking me to lay down on my stomach so he could see my ass.

I did as he asked. I looked back at him to see how he enjoyed the sight.

Bill reached over and started to rub my firm ass cheeks.

"You have such a beautiful ass, Andrea", he said calmly.

I thanked him for the compliment.

It was very soothing as he massaged my ass cheeks. But my face was in the pillow as I enjoyed what he was doing, so I didn't notice that Bill was stroking his cock hard again.

"You know you have a great ass, don't you?" he said.

"Well, yes," I said shyly.

"I also love your big tits," he added. I nodded with a smile.

"Thanks, Bill," I responded.

I should have figured out by now that Bill always talked crude when he was horny. It wasn't too long before he was rubbing his cock against the side of my ass.

"I sure could go for another piece of that tight cunt of yours," he said.

"You wanna screw me again?" I asked.

"I'm a horny guy who doesn't see women like you that often," he replied.

I appreciated the compliment, and reveled in the attention the old stud was giving me.

Bill had already cum twice and the damage was done. Besides, I still had an unsatisfied yearning ache between my legs that told me it wanted more of his big cock.

Still basking from the wonderful fuck he already gave me, I didn't protest when Bill took action to have his way with me again.

"Spread for me," he ordered as he rolling me on my side with my ass towards him.

I obeyed the master cocksman and lifted my leg into the air so he could lay me again. Bill pushed himself down and came up behind me. He slipped the massive prick head into my twat from behind, and quickly stuffed the whole thing into me.

Again my cunt snugly formed around his massive cock, snapping shut on it like a vise as he banged his cock home. I couldn't believe how much I loved having this mans hot prick between my legs. I was instantly excited again.

Bill then started working the big dick in and out of me, as I rested my leg over his. He reached up and started rubbing my tits and squeezing my nipples, causing me to moan like a slut and push back against his thrusts.

"You're such a slut, Andrea," he moaned.

I moaned loudly at his words.

"You love Bill's stiff prick screwing your married cunt, don't you slut?"

My excitement was getting overwhelming. I couldn't hold back much longer. I had to scream out.

"Oh God, make me cum again on that hard cock, you bastard," I shot back.

The nasty dialogue went on, heating up as we fucked.

"Do you want more of Bill's hot seed, sweetheart?"

"Stud me like a bitch in heat," I replied.

The tempo increased, Bill wrapping his leg around mine to increase the force of his banging.

"Andrea, you are a hot fucking slut," he said.

I had to agree.

"God yes, I'm a fucking slut . . . hump me harder you bastard," I impulsively cried out.

Bill brought his hands down from my tits and started rubbing my ass again, running his coarse fingers over my asshole. While it only worked to excite me more, I didn't realize what it was doing to Bill.

As Bill continued to fuck me he roughly asked me a question.

"You ever been fucked up the ass, sweetheart?"

While I was in a deep sex fever, I could still understand the import of his question.

"Oh God, please don't fuck my ass," I begged.

Bill held me tight by the waist and withdrew his slicked up dick from my cunt. I could feel the throbbing cock head probing my backside.

"Aw baby, if I'm going to break you in right you have to feel a hard cock in your ass."

As with my first fucking, again Bill didn't wait to hear my objection. He just rolled me over on my belly, forcefully pushing my face into the pillow. He reached down and wrapped his army around my waist, pulling me up onto my knees.

Bill proceeded to brutally spread my ass checks with his rough hands, positioning the throbbing cock head at my tiny asshole.

"Cherry ass!" he said, "I get to break a cherry ass!"

"No!" I cried.

"Fuck my pussy!" I pleaded.

Bill wouldn't hear of it.

"You stupid cunt," he gloated, "I'm crackin' that virgin ass of yours!!!"

Without mercy, Bill pushed his cock. Unlike my cunt, however, my asshole was not as willing to allow the massive cock head to enter.

"Aghhhhhh," I screamed out with a high-pitched squeal as he pushed his hard cock into my ass.

I tried to pull away from the horny fuck tool, begging and pleading for Bill to spare my virgin asshole.

"It hurts. Please stop Bill. God, please stop!"

My pleas only solidified Bill's intent to fuck my ass, and he pinned my ass down with his hand and pushed again forcing the cock head in.

"Fuck you," he said coldly. "You're a fucking cock tease, and now you're gettin' a big hard cock up your ass!!!"

My head bolted up and a cry of agony spewed forth when my anal flower was split in two. Having succeeded at breaking my asshole open, Bill rammed an inch of his prick in my ass causing me to tightly clutch the pillow below my face from the pain.

I pleaded with the bastard over and over.

"Take it out . . . Oh God Bill, please take it out."

"Shut the fuck up, you stupid bitch," he retorted.

Still not showing any sign of mercy for by plight, Bill pushed in a few more inches of hard cock into my virgin ass.

Bill slowly commented as he cracked my ass open for his and all future cock.

"Fucking'a Andrea . . . your ass . . . sure . . . is . . . tight!"

Taking quick rapid breaths, I clutched the pillow tighter and grit my teeth in order to bear the pain as the old bastard ruthlessly ass raped me.

"Ngggggggh . . .," I grunted as the stud kept forcing more and more of his cock up my ass.

"Ngggggggh . . . God, no!" I cried.

After what seemed to be an eternity, Bill finally had his humongous cock into my ass up to his balls. And then he really gave it to me.

The pain was so overwhelming from the massive throbbing shaft that was stuck deep in my bowels, I could feel my asshole literally spasm around the hot prick.

"How does it feel to have a hard cock in your ass, you cunt?" he asked in a sinister manner.

"It . . . It . . . hurts," I slowly mumbled out.

"Then lets see if we can fix that," he said.

With that, he put his large hands on my waist and lifted my ass off the bed. While I still clutched the pillow, Bill started to deep stroke my asshole.

I felt my mouth drop open and my head fall back the next time Bill's giant cock impaled my tight ass. I started moaning and grunting as he brutally raped my ass, his huge cock slamming into me over and over.

"Rub your clit, slut, it'll make it feel better."

I did as I was told, reaching down between my legs. I rubbed my wet slit furiously, trying to keep my mind off from the pain.

I could feel Bill's balls against my fingers each time he his cock ripped into my ass. Bill was pulverizing my asshole.

At some point in the fucking, the ecstasy grew and mixed with the pain, my head starting to thrash back and forth in like a wanton bitch in heat. My hair why flying!

I was giving in to the bastard, just as he knew I would. I rubbed my gash harder, and I soon grunted as the most powerful orgasm of my life overwhelmed me. I had never had such an intense orgasm in my entire life!

I couldn't believe that I was now freely submitting my ass to this old trucker, allowing him to fuck it as he saw fit. Bill enjoyed it.

"That's it, baby, rub your cunt and you'll be an ass slut before you know it!"

Bill was getting really turned on by the sluttish moan he was drawing from my swooning head. The bastard grabbed me tightly and reamed my virgin ass as hard as could, slamming his hard cock in after each full stroke. His hairy balls kept slapping on my fingers.

My last remaining hole was now wide open.

I kept rubbing my clit as the bastard took my ass. Another powerful orgasm ripped through me and suddenly the pain subsided. Ecstacy was starting to take over.

"My big cock feels good in your ass now, doesn't it you little tramp?"

"Y . . . e . . . s," I grunted.

The crude talk aroused him more.

"Now you love a hard cock in your ass, don't you cunt?"

By now the pain had passed, and I was so deep in ecstasy from the brutal ass fucking that I didn't respond.

Bill withdrew his cock when I didn't answer. In one swift motion, he jammed it up my ass and stopped.

"Don't you, you fucking bitch?" he screamed.

"Yes. Yes. Fuck my ass," I blurted out.

Bill started stroking me again, like a reward for answering him.

"Ahhhh, your ass feels as great as your hot cunt," he groaned.

Bill picked up his tempo, really starting to pile drive me. As he continued to furiously long dick my asshole, my hanging tits bounced around. Bill wanted those, too.

The stud slammed his cock up my ass and stopped again. He reached around to my front and grabbed a tit with each hand. He squeezed them hard, and then twisted my hard nipples in his fingers. The pain was intense, all swirled in my head with the hard cock up my ass.

It was awkward for him, but Bill started to work his cock in and out of my ass again as he continued squeezing my tits. As always, he had commentary.

"These big tits make my cock hard," he groaned as he slowly dicked my ass, ""God, I love these big tits of yours!"

Bill was getting sidetracked, and he knew it. He pulled his body back up and straddled over my ass. He started riding my ass with a renewed intensity. I could tell he was determined to turn me into an ass slut. And at that moment in time, I probably was.

"How bad do you want my cock to stay in your ass?" he demanded.

I just moaned.

"How bad bitch?" he yelled.

I finally succumbed to the intense passion.

"Please, you fucking bastard, don't stop," I said.

"You'd better start begging for this cock bitch," he responded.

When I didn't respond he became angry.

"Beg!" he screamed as he humped my ass harder and harder, slamming his cock into me up to his balls over and over.

"I said beg for my cock bitch!"

My mind was a blur, totally immersed in the ass fucking that was causing these repeated powerful orgasms. That was all I needed to release a torrent.

"Oh God. Please give me your thick cock, you stud."

I moaned and moaned.

"Slam that fat prick up my ass!" I screamed.

Happy with his victory, Bill started laughing as he slowed his strokes. I couldn't stop. I was broken like a horse.

" Take my ass, I'm a fucking slut."

"Ok you horny little bitch," he said coldly as he withdrew his cock and laid next to me on his back.

Bill pulled me over to him and pulled my leg over his body. He held his shaft straight in the air, and guided my asshole to it.

I was about to sit on a cock for the first time in my life!

I slowly squatted on the fat fuckstick, slowly pushing it into me until it was deep in my ass again. I reached down and started rubbing myself again, running my fingernails over his balls as I did so.

"Ohhhh fuck," he moaned in response, "you are such a fucking hot slut!"

I moaned as I started to bounce up and down on his cock, Bill reached up and started playing with my tits again. He pushed my tits together, squeezing them hard. And then he started twisting my nipples again, bringing a new intensity to my orgasms. I swear to God, those nipples must have been more than an inch out.

"Your nipples get harder with a big cock in your ass!" he exclaimed.

His words set me on fire. I was one with the experience, joining him in the sordid talk.

"I love your big cock . . . I love your big cock . . . I love your big cock!" I kept yelling to him over and over as my hair thrashed around from the deep ass fucking.

I just couldn't help myself. What Bill was doing to me turned out to be one of the most gratifying sexual experiences of my entire life. In no time, I was a trained ass slut who wanted more!

Bill likewise was as happy as he could be as he stroked his cock off in my ass. He grabbed my ass and slammed me onto his cock over and over as hard as he could. My asshole was by now gaped wide open.

"Fuck my cock," he yelled, "fuck me back with your tight ass until I cum!"

Bill taught me to draw cum from a cock in my ass. I pushed myself up by my hands and slammed my ass onto his stiff prick as hard as I could. I violently impaled my ass on Bill's cock again and again like a whore!

It was so wanton. Here I was still dressed for work with these new stockings on, driving a massive prick up my ass by myself. There was something about the feeling of the thick prick in my bowels that I didn't want to end. But my ass stud finally had enough.

Bill grunted that he was getting ready to cum. He pushed me off from him to the side, and started jacking another load across my cunt. I looked down to see his jizz splashing my pussy as he rubbed the giant cock head against my cunt lips.

What a stud, I thought! I was amazed that Bill had any cum left in his balls after the two loads he pumped out. While he certainly had a lot less cum, he was still able to squeeze out enough white globs to spread all over my inflamed cunt lips.

When Bill was spent, he reached down with his coarse hand and grasped my pussy. He massaged his wad of cum into my hairy bush like he had earlier. It was so hot as he smeared it across my cunt lips. Pure heaven! That's the only way I can describe it.

"God you're fucking hot Andrea," Bill said as he felt me up, "and those fucking big tits!"

We both laid there for a minute, the passion still running through me as he continued to rub me. I was thinking in disbelief at what had happened that day when Bill suddenly said he had to get moving. Now that his sexual needs were taken care of, I was being thrown out like a common tramp!

I wiped as much cum from myself as I could on his sheets. I was surprised to see blood from my anus on the sheets. I don't know why I was surprised. The man had just sliced my ass open with his big dick.

I fixed my bra, buttoned my blouse, and straightened up my jewelry. I grabbed a comb he had lying around and fixed my hair the best I could.

When I was ready to leave, Bill leaned over and gave me a kiss. I kissed my lover back. Bill then whispered in my ear.

"Andrea, does your husband know you're a slut?"

I looked at him, reality starting to come back. I didn't answer. I just got up and left.

Chapter Six

As I got out of the truck and felt the fresh air on my face, the reality started to sink in.

What had I just done?

There was the pregnancy thing, but I thought I could just go to the doctor for that. I was more worried about how to live without these pleasures that my husband didn't know how to give.

My mind was spinning.

I looked at my car, but decided instead to have another drink. I went back to the bar, and freshened up my makeup and lipstick in the ladies room. I went back to the bar stool and started drinking.

I thought a lot about Bill's filthy talk and the effect it had on me. I thought about the cum, as ass fucking, the . . . I had to figure this out.

It was early afternoon when Bill had finished having his way with me, and I sat and drank for a few hours. I had to figure out what this event meant in my life.

Soon the music started playing as the afternoon happy hour started. I just sat there on the bar stool, drinking beer and thinking.

I noticed men constantly looked at me. I wondered if they could tell that I had just got laid. Little did I know it was how I was dressed.

When I went into the bar, I still had Bill's stockings on. The skirt I wore that day was above my knee, but I didn't notice that you could easily see the top of my stockings when I sat down on the stool. I must have looked like a tramp on the prowl.

There still were not many people in the bar, and most of the men there didn't bother with me despite the sight of my short skirt and stockings. A few men would come up and try to start a conversation, but I just told them to leave me alone. I didn't care for a repeat of Bill at that point.

One man who came up to me didn't like my answer, and he accused me of being stuck up. He was a very big black man who had a muscular body. I was somewhat intimidated by him. I apologized, not knowing that my apology was his cue to sit down next to me.

The man's name was Joe, a 45 year old single man who was much taller than me. Joe was obviously a blue collar worker from his clothes, but that didn't bother me as much as his physique intimidated me.

Joe bought me a beer while we talked for a while about trivial things like our jobs. Eventually, Joe asked me if I was married. I said that I was and showed him my ring. He said he thought so, and that he had noticed my wedding band. I smiled and shrugged my head, telling him that I missed my husband.

Joe asked why I was there alone. I told him my husband was out of town, and that I was trying to figure some things out.

Joe seemed genuinely interested in my state of mind, and he was a lot more gentle than I had imagined when I first saw him. Little did I know that another Bill had walked into my life.

We talked for about an hour when he asked me to dance. The music was all slow, which should have alerted me. But I was feeling pretty tipsy by that time - if not downright drunk - so I really didn't care.

I slipped somewhat when I went to stand up. Joe caught me and put his arm around my waist. He guided me out to the dance floor.

Once we were out on the small dance floor, Joe wrapped his strong arms around me as we slow danced. I instinctively responded by wrapping my arms around the neck, enjoying the feeling of this large man holding me. I kept looking at the contrast of his dark skin to my pale complexion. This was the first time I was ever so close to a black man. I found it to be kind of mesmerizing seeing this difference. I was kind of in a trance with the alcohol, and his obvious growing bulge pressed against me just didn't concern me.

After a few songs, Joe started to make his move. He came closer to me and put his head next to mine. He then started to kiss my neck and ear, but I was in another world and failed to stop him. I just felt the sensation of his tongue running over my skin.

Slowly Joe moved his head up to mine and I looked into his eyes. He then swiftly pressed his lips against mine. With all of the beer I had and the events with Bill, all inhibitions were now gone. I kissed him back.

Joe and I lightly kissed a few times, our tongues gently flickering in my mouth. As we kissed, Joe slowly danced me into a corner where it was dark. Once we were secluded, he nonchalantly reached behind me.

Joe started kissing my neck again as he gently placed his hand on my ass. This strange black man soon ran his hand up my skirt, and in no time he discovered that I had no panties on. I found the sensation of feeling this man's strong hands on my smooth ass cheeks to be incredible.

Joe then moved his hand to my front, all the time keeping his hand up my skirt. I felt him cup his big hands over my bush. He squeezed hard, and I felt his finger freely penetrate my cunt. I gave a slight moan as he entered me.

Joe could definitely tell that I was hot. My slippery lips betrayed me to the black stud.

"You're wet, baby," he said as he continued to kiss my neck.

My pussy started to ignite as he continued to finger me. My body was filled with excitement as this big black man felt me up. I was getting very hot. I turned my head and kiss him again, my tongue eagerly darting into his mouth.

Joe paused and whispered in my ear. He asked me to join him for the evening. My glazed over eyes looked into his as my heart raced. Today I was fully becoming a woman.

I said yes.

Chapter Seven

My husband was out of town with my daughter, but I knew he would eventually try to call me at home. So I called him before I left the bar to deflect the problem. It was a good thing that I did.

Mark and I talked for a few minutes. He said he had tried to call me and was worried when I didn't answer. He also said he tried my cell phone. I explained to Mark that my phone battery had died, and that my girlfriend was having problems and asked me to spend the night with her.

Thankfully, Mark was fine with it. But dear God, I felt so bad. How could I be such a liar to a man I loved so much? Out having sex behind his back . . . and loving it???

I was still feeling bad as I left the bar with Joe. But as bad as I felt, I knew I wanted to have sex with this black man. I had always wondered what having sex with a black man would be like, and at that point I was desperately horny because of Bill.

We decided to take Joe's car and to leave mine in the parking lot. Once I got into his car, Joe immediately moved his hand to my leg. He rode his hand up to the top of my stocking, gently caressing the smooth skin of my thigh. It felt so good to feel his hands rubbing me.

It didn't take Joe long to take more of me. He moved his hand between my legs, and I spread for him. He felt up my pussy, tweaking my cunt lips and pushing his fingers through the hair on my bush. He was driving me absolutely crazy! So I just reached over and felt his raging hard-on through his tight jeans.

When we finally arrived at his place, Joe and I walked in hand-in-hand. We both knew we were going to have sex, but it was kind of odd walking with him like we were girlfriend / boyfriend. The thought didn't last for long, however. My thoughts changed when I walked into the house with him.

I was surprised to see that another man was sitting in the living room. Joe introduced me to Al, his roommate.

Al was sitting on the couch in some old jeans and a white wife-beater t-shirt. He looked to be about the same age as Joe, somewhere in his mid-40's. Where Joe was a light skinned black, Al was as black as night. He was also handsome, well toned, and very muscular.

Al complimented Joe on the beautiful friend he had. I looked at Al with a smile and thanked him. He definitely had the look of someone who wanted to get to know me better.

"Well, Andrea," Al asked, "would you like a beer?

I didn't have time to respond. Joe was waiting for small talk. He pulled my hand and whisked me into his bedroom.

Joe slammed the door shut as soon as I was in the bedroom. He didn't waste any time once he got me where he wanted me. He could obviously tell that I was a horny, married white lady who had proved herself to be an easy mark. We didn't even talk. This was a man who knew what he wanted, and he knew what I wanted. To get laid.

As soon as we were in the room, Joe quickly took me in his strong arms and began kissing me. I kissed my new lover back, my mind still spinning with what had happened with Bill and how sluttish I felt being in this strange black man's bedroom.

Joe and I stood there and kissed for a few minutes. All the time Joe had his hands up my skirt and was rubbing my ass and the top of my stockings.

Eventually, Joe brought his large black hand to the front of me like he did in the bar. He ran his large hand between my legs, just like he did on the dance floor.

Joe stopped for a moment and looked into my eyes. He face was inches from mine as he spoke.

"You're a beautiful woman, Andrea," he said, "let me show you what your husband can't."

I didn't resist as he took my hand and guided me over to his bed. He held my hand as he gestured for me to sit down on the bed. He stood in front of me and looked down.

Joe slowly unzipped his trousers and reached in. He pulled out his soft cock, which was only inches from my face. I was surprised that his cock was still soft after we had just made out. I wondered if it meant he would be able to fuck me for a long time.

As soon as he had his cock out, he said two simple words.

"Suck it."

I looked up the Mandingo stud, and then down to the brown cock that was in front of me. I had never seen a black man's cock before. I was intrigued.

I took Joe's prick in my hand, comparing it to Bill's. It was hard to compare, because it was still flaccid.

I started to jerk Joe's cock, and it started to grow in my hand. I grabbed it tight and jerked it up and down some more. I was amazed at how it continued to grow.

Lusting for the taste of cum after Bill had teased me mercilessly and refused me his, I took the tip of the long black shaft into my mouth and snapped my mouth shut.

As I sucked the shaft, it grew in my mouth until it was as hard as steel. It was an incredible feeling to have this strange, rock-hard black prick in my mouth. I pulled the black cock out to look at it again. I wanted to study this new tool that I was about to enjoy.

I was somewhat saddened to see that Joe's cock was not as thick as Bill's. But it was longer, having to be at least 12" in length. It was truly amazing. While I had heard stories about black men, I never imagined a cock could be this big. It's not something we talk about in Sunday school, after all!

I studied the cock head as I kissed it. It was a massive brown mushroom. It was perfectly shaped, looking like a destroyer of pussy. I knew my cunt lips would soon be opened by it.

I sucked the big brown cock just as Bill had taught me. I sucked the head into my lips and ran my tongue over it. I then stroked the shaft of the giant cock hard and fast, sucking as much of the shaft into my mouth as I could manage.

I licked the cock head some more and rubbed it all over my face as I jerked the shaft. I grew more and more excited as I relished the cock. In my drunken state, the feeling was absolutely exhilarating. I felt like a decadent slut, salivating over this gorgeous cock, and I was loving every minute of it!

Reaching out with my hand, I stroked Joe's hairy ball sac with my fingernails. I then bent down and sucked on his balls. The attention I was giving his cock caused Joe to loudly moan. It seemed that Joe wasn't a talker like Bill, he only moaned.

Joe reached down and completely unbuttoned my blouse, pulling it out of my skirt. He then unsnapped my bra with one hand like a master, and my tits came free.

The black stud proceeded to cup my firm tits with his rough hands and play with my already erect nipples. It was the same as it was with Bill. The attention to my tits made me more horny, and I jerked the big cock harder.

As I grew more comfortable with this strange new prick, I decided to give Joe a little more. I started rubbing the big black cock all over my tits, popping the head into my mouth every few seconds. I then slowly worked the long throbbing stick into my throat. It was a little hard at first, but I relaxed as Bill so sternly instructed me.

In no time, I was lunging forward to stroke this big fucker's prick off in my throat. I couldn't get all of it down there, but I tried with everything I had!

It was too much for Joe.

Apparently worried that he was a "one-shot" man, he grabbed my head in his hands and pulled his cock out of my throat.

"You're going to make me cum," he said.

I smiled at him and licked my lips.

"But not before I fuck that nice white pussy of yours," he then added.

I knew then that my cunt was about to be ravished by the second big cock it found that day. I decided I wasn't going to fight it this time.

Joe backed up from me and unbuckled his pants, getting ready to mount his prize. He kicked off his shoes and dropped his trousers. I could tell from the way he unbuckled his pants that it wouldn't be long before I was mounted. This black stud was horny for a beautiful white woman, and he was about to take his prize.

I had no idea what to expect. This was only the third man I had ever been with in my life, and my first black man.

Once Joe was undressed, he walked back to the bed and just pushed me backwards. He climbed onto the bed as I laid on the bed, my legs slightly spread for him. Joe wasted no time running his hand up my thigh and to my cunt. I grabbed his cock as I instinctively spread my legs wide for my stud.

Joe didn't put a lot of effort into foreplay. He could tell I was wet and ready. After a few short minutes of kissing me and feeling me up, he wrapped his arms around me and pulled me further onto the bed. Soon my head was resting on his pillow.

The horny black bastard wasn't wasting any time for his piece of white ass, I thought.

Joe now had me flat on my back and pinned down with his chest. He reached down and hiked up my skirt to my waist. It was a strange feeling. Here I was, exposed from the waist down to this stranger, this black man, this stud. But I was so horny. I just wanted him to take me and use me right there and then.

Joe quickly rolled on top of me, using his powerful legs to force my legs apart to accommodate him. He moved himself between my spread legs and held his torso up with his muscular arms. He started kissing me again as he mounted me. I could feel his stiff prick probing between my legs.

This cocksman didn't even need to guide his cock. The head found its mark on its own as he slowly pushed it into my cunt. Oh God, the feeling of being opened by this huge black cock! My mouth slowly opened as I looked at him, a slight moan escaping from my lips.

Joe pushed the throbbing cock head in, my pussy readily accepting it after Bill opened me up with his big cock head. And then all of a sudden, in one rapid thrust, Joe slammed the whole length of 12" black shaft into my wet cunt.

I loudly gasped when the cock forcefully split my cunt open and deeply impaled me. I could feel my cunt snugly form around this new hot prick. I couldn't believe how deep the fucker was in my pussy. Joe's cock was longer than Bill's, giving my pussy a whole new sensation. I thought the bastard had to be in my womb. And I absolutely loved it.

My head was spinning again. Here I was getting laid for the third time that day, this time by a big black stud. I knew my eggs were about to be doused in cum again, but I just didn't care. I just wanted to get laid.

Joe then started to really give it to me. He slow fucked me to start, giving me long deep strokes of his shaft which put me in heaven. I looked down as Joe slowly worked his prick off in my cunt. He had himself propped up by his hands, giving me a bird's eye view of what he was doing to me. I was absolutely mesmerized by the sight of my pink pussy lips enveloping this massive black pole that was stroking through my cunt.

Yes, I wanted it. All I cared about was getting my cunt stroked by this muscular black stud. I wrapped my upward leg around Joe's waist and slammed my hips towards my fucker to match his every stroke. I wanted to feel every inch of that hot prick as it stroked off inside my cunt.

Joe then brought his free hand under my ass and grabbed my ass cheek tight. He proceeded to fuck me in quick rapid strokes, using his hand on my ass to make sure that he was thrusting as deep into me as he could. The feeling was indescribable

As Joe used my cunt to stroke off his humongous cock, it is set off a series of intense orgasms in me. I was cumming over and over, causing me to share my emotions.

"Oh God," I kept crying.

Joe stroked me faster as I sucked on his earlobe.

"Your cock is so big!" I moaned in his ear.

This stud wasn't a talker. He just grunted with each stroke into my cunt.

Every now and then, Joe would release his grip on me ass. He would look down to see what his tool was doing to me. It really was quite a sight to behold. I heard myself moaning loudly the whole time. I was a bitch in heat!

Al had to hear my moans, as the bedroom was right off from the living room. I gave it little thought though, because the sensations in my cunt were too overwhelming to ignore.

Joe must have stroked me for 20 minutes. After Joe had thoroughly drilled my cunt with his black cock, he slowed and looked down at me.

He asked me a question.

"Are you using protection?" he asked.

The thought had slipped my mind, between the beer and being so caught up in the fucking I was getting. Forgetting what happened when I told Bill, I thoughtlessly answered that I hadn't.

The lesson was given to me again.

It must be something about men when they think they have a chance to knock a woman up. All my comment did was inflame Joe's black passions.

Joe started to grunt as he slowed the temp of his strokes. He would pull the whole 12" rod out of me and then slam it in all the way to his balls with as much force as he could.

Joe continued with the slow, hard, long strokes about five more times, grunting the whole time. I could feel his balls slapping my ass and his back started to tense. I knew he was close.

"Ohhh fuck . . . I'm . . . going to cum . . . knock . . . knock you up!"

With that he started to cream deep between my legs, intent on implanting me with his bastard child.

Joe wasn't alone. His statement of fact coupled with the feeling of having this black man buried deep between my widely spread legs caused me to cum uncontrollably. I was surprised when I heard myself encourage him.

"Please, cum in me," I cried, "I want to feel your black cum inside of me!"

Joe finally stopped when his cock was buried as deep in my uterus as he could go. He held it there while the shaft jerked a hot wad of black seed deep into me, painting my eggs with his hot cum.

I could feel the big black cock swell and his nut sack spasm as he sprayed at least four jets of cum inside me. I couldn't believe the feeling. Just as it was with Bill, I could feel the hit seed as the hard cock pressed it into my cunt walls. It was so hot and so silky smooth. And I could feel it slosh around and leak down my ass crack as Joe slow stroked me.

Once Joe was sure that his balls were completely empty, he stroked my cunt for a few a few minutes more as his cock went soft. He collapsed on me, panting, as I rubbed his smooth muscular ass cheeks.

I was sad.

I felt that the stud let me down.

I wasn't satisfied.

I was hoping Joe would get hard again as I caressed his ass, so he could service me a little more like Bill had done. I gently scratched his ass cheeks with my nails as he lay collapsed on me. I hoped . . .

My hopes were dashed.

It wasn't long before my clinching cunt caused Joe's limp cock to pop out of my cunt. And then he was done.

"I'll be right back," he said as he climbed off from me, and he left the room.

Chapter Eight

I laid there waiting for Joe to come back, feeling his sticky cum seep from my pussy. Having been introduced to the joy of cum by Bill, I curiously reached down and picked up a few wad of cum with my fingers. I rubbed it in into my lips like lip balm.

The taste of the black man's cum mixed with lipstick was wonderful. The feeling of it on my lips kept me hot and excited.

I hoped Joe would come back soon to finish what he started. After a few minutes of playing with myself, however, I was shocked when Al walked in totally naked from the waste down, smirking as he watched me lap up Joe's cum.

There stood this black stud in his wife-beater t-shirt. I couldn't help but notice how handsome and muscular this black man was.

I pulled my legs up to cover my exposed pussy, and I covered my chest with my hands. I looked at Al and snarled, "What the hell are you doing?"

This new black stud walked over to the bed and sneered.

"Joe told me to help myself to a piece of the married white slut he just boned."

I couldn't believe what I was hearing.

"Yes ma'am, he promised me a nice tight white wife's cunt," he gloated.

Joe never gave any indication that he was like that. It all seemed romantic with him. I was so wrong.

Al came closer to the bed, his limp black cock dangling in front of him. Here I was comparing cocks again. In one exciting day, I was becoming a cock critic!

Al's cock was exceptionally dark, and it was quite long considering that it was still flaccid. The dark cock head was also quite large. I knew this prick would be something when it became rock hard.

"Well, you wanna suck my nigger cock sweetheart?" he asked with a grin.

I looked at him in disbelief, my body still hot and aching for cock.

"I'd be happy to pump a load of hot cum down that pretty little throat of yours," he continued as he reached out and stroked my hair with his hand.

I was absolutely speechless from the spectacle of this naked black man boldly prancing into Joe's bedroom expecting to score with me after I just had sex with his roommate. I couldn't believe this total stranger just walked into his roommate's bedroom naked, expecting to get serviced. What the hell was happening?

Al capitalized on my stunned state.

Having heard no objection from me, Al lifted one of his legs onto the bed. He brought his dangling limp cock over my face. He squatted a bit and let his giant cockhead rest on my lips.

I guess I was a whore-in-training at that point in the day. I had so much cock please me, it was instinctive for me to just open my mouth to accept it.

My body was betraying me. I was still so damned horny from the partial fucking Joe had given me and the taste of the cum I had just licked up.

Feeling the last inhibitions flow from my being, I sucked the black prick into my mouth, snapping my lips shut once I had the massive cock head trapped. I was a cock slut who wanted more cock to suck, so I submitted to the huge black bastard who wanted to take me to service his prick.

As I sucked on the soft cock, I was surprised as it filled my mouth when it grew hard and started to throb. This cock was on a stallion. Al's cock was a little longer than Joe's -- about 14" glorious inches -- and a lot thicker than Bill's. I couldn't even begin to wrap my hand around this dark black telephone pole. It blew my mind. How could any cock be this big, I wondered. I was enthralled by the enormous black rod.

I quickly realized that if Bill and Joe hadn't completely opened me up, Al would certainly finish the job with this log. God, how I wanted to be opened up by this magnificent cock!

I sucked on the humongous cock as I laid on my back. I enjoyed working it until it was rock hard.

Al came up on the bed and straddled over my chest. His balls rested on my tits as his cock was being serviced. He reached down to run his hands up my thighs and over my cum-drenched cunt.

Unlike Joe, Al was a talker.

"You got a sweet white pussy bitch. I can't wait to stick my cock in it."

The filthy, sordid talk had the same effect on me as it did when Bill said it. It turned me lose. I sucked on the cock harder, trying to get it into my throat to no avail. I wanted this prick to fuck my throat like a cunt, but it was just too thick.

Al knew I was trying to deep throat him.

"You fucking white slut . . . you better get my big nigger cock down your throat."

I furiously rubbed the ball sac, cupping Al's massive balls in my hand. I kept trying to impale my face on this massive fuck rod.

"Suck my cock you bitch, you fucking white whore."

"You'll get your cum, you little white slut . . . the night is far from over for you bitch."

As Al was remaking me into his whore, Joe came back and sat in a chair.

"Told you the bitch can suck cock, didn't I?" he said to Al.

"Mother fucker, this white bitch must be a pro," Al replied.

"I don't think so," Joe went on, "she's said she's not using any protection."

That seems to be the magic statement that instantaneously makes men twice as horny. Al looked down at me and said in the most crude voice imaginable.

"Is that right, you fucking bitch? Did your fucking husband send you out to get a cunt full of black seed?"

The whole idea of becoming impregnated by these vile black studs made the excitement grow. I could feel my pussy drip from the thought of it. I gave a sluttish moan in response to his question.

That was all Al needed to hear. Any thought of getting the load of cum down my throat that he had promised was now out of the question.

Knowing the prospect of impregnating this married white woman, it was clear that Al was intent on creaming between my legs. His cock was raging hard, ready to deliver.

Al pulled his long, fat cock out of my mouth and brutally grabbed my arms. He yanked me off of the bed, literally pulling me onto the floor.

"On your knees bitch," he commanded.

I thought maybe Al was going to splash my face with his hot spunk. I was wrong. The bastard was getting ready to stud me.

I obeyed, getting down on my hand and knees. Al quickly came around to the back of me. I was going to get laid by this brutal black bastard.

I submitted my cunt to this horny black bastard, raising my ass in anticipation. I knelt on the floor facing the bed, resting my arms up over the side. The hair from my bush dangled down between my legs, enticing the horny bastard. I just waited in anticipation for the black seed that was about to be pumped up my cunt.

"That's it baby," he said coldly, "raise that nice white ass for Al!"

I braced myself and grabbed the sheets with my hands, knowing that this man was determined to get a good piece of me. Al kneeled behind me and pushed my head down into the bed as he groped my cunt.

I felt the throbbing cock at the entrance of my quivering pussy. My slick cunt lips were poised to be opened by the massive head of Al's horny prick. And I was so ready!

"Here's your nigger seed, bitch," he said as he jammed that massive cock head into me.

My cunt had never been opened by such a massive prick. I felt the head split me open.

"Ohhhhhh," I cried out as the giant head parted my cunt lips and imbedded itself in me.

I gripped the sheets tighter and pressed my face into them. My cunt lips now parted, Al ruthlessly pushed the black mushroom head deeper into me. My head bolted backwards and my mouth popped open.

"Ahhhhh . . . fuck," I cried out again with a deep sluttish groan.

"Goddamn your tight!" he said in joy.

"Oh fuck!" he moaned, "a nice tight piece of white pussy!"

While I was lose from all the fucking and cum from that day, the black fuck stick was just too fat. It was like a fucking log. It had to be thicker than a baseball bat. The friction was keeping Al from pushing it in as easily as he thought he could.

"I'll take care of that tight cunt for you, bitch. Would you like that?"

"Oh fucked!" I cried out.

"You ready to get laid again, bitch?" he asked coldly.

I started to beg him to take me, enticing him as best I could.

"God, I want you to lay me!"

"Then spread those sweet legs nice and wide, baby, cause my prick is pretty thick and you're tight as hell!"

"Go ahead, you black bastard, open me up!"

Al loved it, gripping my waist tightly for better leverage.

"Fucking right I will, cunt, you'll have one sloppy hole when I through with you."

Holding me incredibly tight, Al split my insides apart as he ruthlessly plunged the rest of his thick black bone into my tight cunt in one swift stroke. I pressed my face harder into the sheets, but my head turned and my mouth uncontrollably opened with a groan as Al stretched my cunt to accommodate his fat prick.

"Ahhhh fuck," I said again as my twat formed around the massive intruder.

My pussy was being reshaped by the sheer size of the massive fucker.

"Fuck me with that big black cock," I said as I turned around to kiss this big buck nigger.

Al kissed me back passionately, his big calloused hands caressing my ass cheeks. He then set his mind to the task at hand.

Now deeply impaled to the hilt by his hot cock and begging for it to boot, the fucker began to savagely pump me with his massive black rod. I could tell from his expressions of lust on his face that he was totally loving the feeling of having his cock buried between my spread legs.

Having succeeded in smashing into my cunt, Al removed his arms from my waist and grabbed my hips. Then he started working his cock off. I screamed out from the ecstacy of being studded by this strange black bastard.

"Stroke that big black cock off in my pussy, you bastard!"

"Mmmm," he groaned.

Al slowly ground his hot fuck stick in and out of my cunt. This man was deep inside my cunt, and I could feel myself stretched all the way to my asshole. He now braced himself to give me a fucking I'd never forget.

Al started with slow deep strokes, drawing sultry groans from me with each one. I felt like I came each time he thrust that massive hot fuck stick into me, the cock head banging deep inside me. I was going insane from the stud service this old black man was giving to me.

"Ahhhh fuck, your prick is so hard!" I said again, enjoying the feel of the thick black cock stroking through my cunt.

"Your tight white cunt needed a big stiff one!" he responded.

I guess something in me wanted this black man to screw me senseless.

"Pound my horny white cunt, you bastard!"

I figure I was unconsciously looking forward to the brutal cunt pounding this dirty bastard would surely give me.

Sure enough, my Mandingo lover delivered. He immediately began the most unbelievable long dicking my tender white cunt has ever felt, my legs shaking each time the massive black cock head banged home.

My whole body started convulsing as Al savagely hammered me. I felt like a porn star being using by that big black cock.

Al was now humping my raw cunt like a dog in heat. I felt like a wild woman taking that black horse cock, whorishly moaning as Al studded me.

And enjoy me he did.

Al went on nonstop, slamming me harder with each wicked statement, as though debasing me with filth gave him the same kind of perverted erotic joy that it gave me. It's amazing I met two men who acted the same way with women in the same night!

"Take my black cock, you fucking bitch!"

"You're a hot little slut!"

"You love my thick nigger prick, don't you bitch?"

"You're asshole's next, you fucking slut, I'm gonna split it wide open!"

"You enjoyin' getting humped by a big black prick, bitch?"

"I'm gonna pump your tight cunt full of black seed, bitch!"

"I'm gonna knock you up with my nigger seed, you white tramp!"

"Damn, I'm gonna cream between your gorgeous legs!"

Each time Al's debasing profanity came out it sank into my ears, just as it had with Bill. Al brought me to a new level of ecstasy with the raunchy talk, and I made each vile statement a part of my soul. I was becoming one with it, repeatedly yelling out "YES!" to each new statement Al spit out at me as I submitted to the fucker's unbridled lust.

The feeling of the colossal black prick violently stroking through my battered cunt without mercy with my skirt hiked up was too much for me. I succumbed to lust I had never known before while this fuck monster stroked his prick off in my pussy. I pushed back to meet the fucker's every thrust, openly submitting my cunt to anything he wanted to do with it.

Al was also lost in lust, getting ready to inject his man seed deep into me. By that time I was ready to do anything to help the bastard fill me with his sperm.

Our thoughts must have crossed.

Al brutally gave me one last tremendous lunge of his hot, black prick, and his great cock head finally erupted a load of gooey cum deep up my cunt. When the horse cock began to flood my cunt with nigger seed, I screamed out from the orgasm it caused.

"Ahhhh," Al moaned, "you're so fucking tight!"

Our cum mixed deep in my fertile womb, the black bastard pumping what must have been a gallon of hot seed that I could feel as it stuck to the walls of my womb. I could feel each scalding spurt as it splashed against my insides. My eggs were truly soaked by this big black stud, and I didn't care.

I just wanted this hard cock to keep taking and using me, making me feel like a real woman with each blast of hot spunk. I felt so sexy, so decadent. I didn't want it to end.

I had no idea it wasn't even close to ending.

Chapter Nine

All of the filthy talk and the sight of a beautiful white woman getting royally fucked obviously perked Joe back up. After Al dismounted me, Joe came over and told me I was a "wonderful little lady."

Yeah right, you bastard!

Joe helped me to my feet and gently sat me down on the bed. He climbed on the bed and laid down next to me, his back up against the headboard. He held up his erect cock straight up and gestured for me to come over to service it. I didn't need much enticing as I bent over.

My head reached between this 45-year old strange black man's legs. I went down on him. I took the stiff prick in my hand, and jerked it hard a few times. It looked so wonderful and tempting. I couldn't help myself. I impaled myself on the beautiful cock and started to deep throat it with reckless abandon. It was quite easy after having used Al's cock to open up my throat.

Al left when I started doing this, commenting as he left.

"This fucking whore is hot!"

I pulled myself onto the bed and kneeled between Joe's legs. I bent over and went to work on the stiff prick. I quietly slurped on

Joe's cock like a wild woman for about 10 minutes. I licked the shaft up and down and popped it into my throat every few seconds. It was no problem taking about half of this 12" cock in my throat by this time.

I loved hearing Joe's moans of joy. I felt like a true whore servicing a john! Joe just rubbed my hair as I worked on his tool, loving the taste of this black cock meat.

I lifted the big cock and started to lick the hairy ball sac, gently sucking each ball into my mouth. I started to rake my long fingernails over his balls as I sucked. This caused Joe to moan loader, the moment being broken with Al's return.

"Well, bitch, you remember I told you your ass was next?"

Actually, I had forgotten. With the fucking and all, everything went so fast when Al told me what a slut I was and what he was going to do to me.

As I continued to lick Joe's cock, my mind quickly went to the thought of how big Al was and what it would do to my ass. Al was the longest and thickest bastard who had me that day, and I remembered the initial pain Bill caused me.

I stopped licking and looked back towards Al. He was climbing on the bed, heading for my ass with his stiff telephone pole sticking straight out.

"Al, I don't know, you're kind of big," I said with hesitation.

"Kind of big?" he replied. "I call this King Cock, and it loves breaking white ass."

Al moved closer, pulling my ass up so I was upright on my knees. He placed his humongous black battering ram on my palpitating anus, His words sent fear into me, and I could barely get the words out.

"Al, please don't hurt me."

His response was swift and without mercy as he proceeded to break into my ass.

"Fuck you bitch . . . Take my black cock!"

Joe, who was lonely for my probing tongue, didn't allow me to beg for mercy again. He pulled my head towards his crotch and jammed his black cock into it.

Al then proceeded to rawdog my ass with his black hose. He pushed the throbbing black mushroom head against my asshole. It gave a little because Bill had so thoroughly fucked it, but it was still tight after hours of relaxation.

My head bolted back from an initial jolt of pain, and my gaping mouth cried out. The huge head popped into my ass, and I screamed out.

Al pushed harder, intent on drawing blood from my ripped open ass.

"Aggggggh . . .", I cried.

"Fucking scream bitch, it ain't gonna do no good," Al said as he grabbed my waist and pushed a few inches in.

I started turning my head back and forth, crying out in rapid succession as my asshole spasmed on the massive black prick. I couldn't believe another man was raping my ass the same day it was virgin.

"Aggggh . . . Aggggh . . . Aggggh . . ."

Al loved the response, and he continued to work his huge cock into my ass.

"Feel my big black cock in your lily white ass, you cunt," he said, as he worked it in further.

"Aggggh . . . Aggggh . . . Aggggh . . ."

"Tell your husband there's nothing like a hard black cock stuck in your tight white ass," Al said as he drove his cock home.

"Aggggh . . . Aggggh . . . Aggggh . . ."

The rotten bastard finally got his entire rock hard shaft deep into my bowels, and then he started to really give it to me.

"Andrea, your white slut ass belongs to me," Al said, as he withdrew his entire cock.

The massive cock head then dislodged, causing my asshole to snap shut. Al quickly jammed his thick prick back into my ass to the hilt, violently thrusting until his heavy balls whacked up against my cunt. I could actually hear them slap against me.

"I'm going to open this cunt's asshole once and for all," he said to Joe as he again withdrew the entire cock until my anal ring snapped shut.

Al was methodical . . . and merciless. He swiftly jammed his hard cock all the way back up my ass until his balls slapped against my cunt again. He was ripping my tight asshole ring wide open.

Al did this about a half a dozen times, each time with a new vile statement of what he was doing to my ass. And each time he drew wicked grunts from me.

"You won't be able to sit for a week!"

"Aggggh . . . Aggggh . . . Aggggh . . ."

"You tell your husband that a big buck nigger fucked his wife's ass raw!"

"Aggggh . . . Aggggh . . . Aggggh . . ."

"I am going to rip your tight ass open!"

"Aggggh . . . Aggggh . . . Aggggh . . ."

Each time he fully withdrew and immediately re-impaled me with his thick shaft drew a deep, whorish moan from my lips, indicating final submission to anything this man wanted to do to me.

I have to say, Al's ass breaking technique was simply awesome. I gave in to the lust. My head began to swoon and drool escaped from my gaping mouth as Al's massive cock head rolled through my guts.

Al loved it. He obviously loved breaking white women into the joy of black anal sex!

"That's it, cunt! Moan for my big black cock, you horny white bitch!"

And I did. I moaned like a whore as he ass fucked me.

Throughout the ordeal, Joe was thoroughly enjoying the show. I had my hand on his cock and was jacking it hard as Al took my ass. I found myself using the hard fuck stick to balance myself from the furious ass pounding Al was giving to me.

When Al thought I was lose enough for a good hard ass banging, he started to slam me with quick, long strokes. I reached down between my legs as Bill had taught me and started playing with my clit with my free hand.

Al was quick to notice.

"You fucking slut, you love having a big nigger cock stroking your ass."

I responded by reaching further back, running my fingernails over his nuts as they slammed up against my cunt.

"Ah yeah, baby" he moaned as he stopped to enjoy the sensation, "rub my nuts!"

An orgasm came over me with the comment. I was on fire with that massive black cock deep up my ass. I leaned down and bobbed my head down on Joe's cock, briskly taking damn near the whole 12" deep into my throat.

Al reached down and started grabbing my tits, He squeezed them as his cock was lodged in my ass. My ass clinched tight on the black rod.

Al then brought his hand over to my right ass cheek with his left hand, squeezing it tightly. He gave his a hard slap and then started relentlessly long dicking my ass.

The black stud slammed that horse cock into me much harder than Bill ever had. Stroke after stroke, the black bastard slammed his massive 14" cock into my bowels, lewd statement flowing from his mouth the whole time he buttfucked me.

"You love black prick in your ass . . ."

"Married white cunt craves hot nigger cock up her ass . . ."

"Can't get enough black cock for her tight white ass . . ."

"Moan for my black prick, you fucking white cunt . . ."

All I could do was return deep, whorish moans as I thrashed my swooning head around.

The whole spectacle drove Al wild, much more so than when he had fucked me. The more he talked and the more I moaned, the harder he slammed my willing ass. I could tell that it was quite a show for Joe, the man who seduced me and brought me home to Al.

Yes, Joe was getting overwhelmed by all of the dirty talk and the feeling of having his cock continuously lodged deep in my throat. He decided to change the situation.

"Al, I want her cunt," he said to his roommate.

Al complied immediately, picking me up with his huge hands with his cock stuck deep in my ass. He flipped over on his back, his arms tightly around my body.

I was soon on my back with this big black man underneath me, his cock deep in my ass. Joe got up and got between my legs. He took his cock and started working it into my cunt.

I thought I had experienced it all, but a new pleasure I could never even imagine opened up for me. Double penetration!

Joe pushed his long cock into my cunt, propping himself over me by his arms. When Joe was in as deep as his balls, I could feel Al start to stroke me as best he could from underneath me.

Joe started to stroke my cunt, and the feeling of this double fucking overtook me. I could feel my eyes rolling in my head from the intense feeling of these two hard cocks steam-rolling through my holes.

"Give me your black cocks you bastards," I screamed.

Al loved it.

"Service these cocks, white bitch!" he laughed.

I sent me further over the edge.

"I'm a slut, I'm a horny slut. Fuck the shit out of me!" I screamed.

The fuckers obliged, double humping in front and in back. They filling me like I had never been filled before. And I didn't want it to stop!

Al's head was next to mine, and he ran his tongue into my ear.

"You're a fuck whore," he whispered in my ear, "you live to service black cock."

"Yes," I responded, "I service black cock . . . Give it to me . . . Give it to me."

The bastards double fucked me for about five intense minutes, and then it got to be too much for them. Joe, who was enjoying his second piece of ass, was the first to exclaim that he was going to cum.

I cried out, "Please cum on my face, please, please, you promised me cum."

Joe didn't answer, he just got off of me.

Al pushed my body off from his and pushed me onto my back.

Joe was next. I could tell he was ready to blast when he started moaning loudly. He brought his cock close to my face, and I opened my mouth and stuck out my tongue.

Joe popped the head of his black cock into my mouth and started to blow his wad. Even though he already blew a wad up my cunt, he still had plenty more deep in his balls. It was no time before my mouth had cum.

I swallowed as fast as I could. Cum built up on my lips each time I closed my mouth to swallow. I couldn't help but wonder, how could any man cum so much?

As I closed my mouth to swallow the last of the fresh cum, Joe milked every last drop from his cock. A string of cum ran from the tip of his cock head down to my lips. I pushed out my tongue and swirled it into my mouth.

"Look at that fucking horny cunt swallow cum!" Al exclaimed at the sight.

"She sure is one hot wife!" Joe responded.

When Joe was finally finished, I ran my hand across my lips and cheeks, collecting as much as I could before lapping it up. I was reveling in the amount of cum I had just earned, and savored the sweet taste of the thick, milky sperm. Yes sir, I did love cum.

I was about to get a lot more.

Chapter Ten

When Al and Joe were cumming so profusely on my face, I had heard the door to the house open the some people come in. I was too caught up in what I was doing to think much about it or to care.

When my fuckers were done plastering my face with seed, Al broke the news to me.

"Hey, bitch, I called a few friends when you were sucking Joe off. I told you the night was far from over."

This horny black bastard wanted to turn me into a fuck queen!

Slowly reality started to come back, although I was clearly still in heat. Joe, the gentle one, looked down at me and asked very nicely if I wanted the party to continue. I told him I didn't know.

Al replied "Come on, bitch, you know you're loving this. What the fuck? There's only a couple of them."

While crude, Al was right. I was already deep into infidelity, and I was enjoying myself immensely. In fact, what they did to me made my cunt ache for more cock. I was drunk with sex, and I was in heat. I felt that I wanted to, no, needed to service more black cock. I really didn't care if he let his friends gang bang me.

I didn't want to get killed though.

"I don't want to get hurt or do anything weird," I said.

"Don't worry baby," Al promised, "I'll take care of you."

I looked at Al and said that I would give it a try if I could end it whenever I wanted. Both men agreed.

Al smiled and kissed me.

"You really are a horny slut, Andrea, you'll never stop."

Al wanted to tease his friends with Joe's lucky find, so he told me to go into the bathroom to clean up and primp. He told me to come out "looking like the lady I used to be."

I told him that I needed my purse, which I had left in the living room when I had first come in.

Al put on a rob and went to get it for me. I could hear the yelps of joy in the next room after he had left.

My mind was swimming in unabated lust. I hoped I knew what I was doing.

Al came back with my purse, and I went into the bathroom to freshen up. I had so much dried cum on me, it wasn't going to be easy.

Al followed me into the bathroom and watched as I got ready. He made lewd comments the entire time. I loved it!

I fixed my bra and buttoned my blouse. It had dried nigger cum all over it.

"You got great tits, Andrea."

I tucked the blouse into my skirt. I was surprised to see patches of blood on my skirt from the ruthless ass raping Al gave me with that massive black cock of his.

As I pulled up the stockings Bill gave to me, Al offered a comment.

"Stockings make for a great fuck outfit, huh baby?"

I smiled as I cleaned his cum off of my face, licking it off from my necklace.

"Don't go nuts, baby, were gonna paint your face with cum anyway."

A few large wads of cum were in my hair, so I brushed them in so you couldn't see it.

"You like it in the hair, baby?"

I smiled with that one too, because I did!

I continued by fixing up my makeup and putting on more of my red lipstick.

"Christ, you're hot Andrea," Al said.

I kicked my hair back as I sprayed perfume on my neck. I walked close to him so he could smell the fragrance.

"Does your old man know what you do?"

I ignored the question, and finished my preparations. Tighten the shoe strap and straighten the ankle bracelet. Surprised it hasn't broken yet, I thought.

"Baby, you're in for the time of your life!"

With that last comment, I raised my hands to Al's face. I gave him a big kiss and hugged him. I whispered in his ear.

"I'm you're slut tonight, Al, and if you ever want me to come back you'll manage your boys well."

I think he got the message.

Al smiled, took my hand, and led me to the living room. I was about to pull my first train.

When we arrived in the living room, I was surprised to see seven new black men. I guessed that they ranged in age from 30 to 60. The men yelped when I came in, cheering. They each had a beer in their hand.

I looked at Al, placed my hand on his chest and asked so everyone could hear.

"Baby, you think I can have a beer?" I asked in an innocent tone.

That made all the men cheer again.

Al told one of the men – Bobby – to throw him a beer. Al caught it with one hand as Bobby tossed it over to him. He opened and handed it to me.

"Here you go sweetheart," he said as if we were lovers.

I was thirsty as hell from the cum, so I took a deep drink. The crowd of men cheered again. Al then introduced me to the men.

There was Bobby who threw the beer. He was a fat man about my height. He was in his early 40's.

There was Jimmy -- he was tall and older, in his mid-60's.

There was Fred -- he was of medium build, maybe in his 50's.

There was Alvin -- a stocky man I would say in his early 30's who just sat quietly in a corner.

There was Eddie – another man also in his 50's.

And there was Dave -- a very tall man in his late 30's.

I was surprised to see a handsome young boy named Nick – let's say he was 18 so I don't get accused of statutory rape!

Finally, there was Joe and Al, for nine men in all. My train had 9 cars. What a night this was going to be.

Al thoroughly enjoyed introducing me to his friends. He held me in front of him, with his arms wrapped around me like I was his prized girlfriend. He beamed like a proud father.

What Al told the group of men was kind of embarrassing, but I should have guessed Al would do this.

"This is Andrea. She's a banker, so make your deposits here boys! Oh, and she's married too, so let's not let her husband down. There's no going back for him! But let's not leave any marks on the lady. Don't want her old man to hurt her!"

The men were all yelling and cheering as Al reached over and kissed me. I wrapped my arms around his neck and kissed him back passionately.

Al then stopped kissing me to continue his announcement.

"This little lady is a dream, she loves to fuck and suck, and can't get enough in her ass. She begged me for a gang bang, and I couldn't let her down."

Al then looked at me and kissed me. I whispered in his ear.

"What about some cum, baby," I asked.

Oh shit! I meant for my face! But it reminded him.

"All she asks is that you save at least one load for her face. We can do that, huh guys? One last thing, almost forgot. This little lady is ripe. No protection. She wants you boys to make sure she's knocked up before she leaves, right baby?"

Oh, what the fuck! Can't get any lower than this, I though. So, I looked back at him, and smiled at him with a devilish look.

"Yes baby, I wanna get knocked up by your friends."

Al smiled and kissed me again as the room went absolutely wild. Damn! Every black man in the room now being intent on impregnating my fertile womb with their black bastard child.

I looked at Al and whispered in his ear again.

"Don't let them hurt me," I said.

"Don't worry, I'll be right here," he whispered.

Al then took control of the show.

"Ok boys, we have to do this orderly. Can't kill the woman,." he said.

He walked me over to the sofa and started to sit down.

"This is my slut, and I want you to treat her right. You can say whatever you want -- she knows what she is and she loves to hear it -- and you can fuck her anywhere you want and as hard as you want, but don't hurt her or you'll answer to me."

Thank god, the bastard listened to me. Al then reached over to a side table and turned on a radio.

"Ok fellas," he said, "enjoy the show!"

He then looked at me.

"Strip," he commanded with one single word.

I was incredibly excited about what was happening, and I loved the attention these men gave to me. For the first time in my life, I felt incredibly beautiful.

I knew I could make each of these men as happy as they could make me. I was intent on giving them the best night of their lives!

I danced back and forth in front of them, making sure my long shapely legs were well noticed as I hiked my skirt up. I tossed my head so my hair would fly as I walked up to each man and rubbed my soft white hands against their unshaven black faces.

Thinking of the cum these nine ball sacs held, I stopped in front of the group and slowly licked my lips as I started to unbutton my blouse.

I got half way down when I noticed how much Al was smiling. I thought I'd make him smile more.

I must have been drunk! I couldn't believe what I did next. I held out my wedding ring for all to see. It would cost them a price.

"I'm a married lady boys, so I need a reason to strip naked for a bunch of horny black men. Let me see some black cock."

The men cheered, all but one complying with my request. For some reason, Alvin just watched with a cold look on his face.

Some of the men didn't wait for further instructions or encouragement, they just stripped. I had to go up to two of them and rub my hands over their crotches.

And poor Nick. He looked so shy and reserved, like he wanted to do it just to show the others that he was a man. I felt sorry for the boy.

I looked around at the room full of growing black snakes, the atmosphere teeming in anticipation of hot sex with a married white woman. Most of the cocks were still soft, but a few were already rock hard. I could see that I wouldn't be disappointed.

I finished unbuttoning my blouse and dropped it to the floor. I walked up to Al and bent over to push my tits into his face. I squeezed them together and thrust them into his face so the material of the bra was just off from his lips.

"Please help me baby," I asked.

Al loved it. He reached out and unstrapped my bra. It fell open and my tits fell out. Al placed his hands on the sides of my tits and started to suckle as the men cheered. As I stood up, you could hear the sound of his lips becoming unstuck from my nipples.

I dropped the bra. I started to rub my tits and tweak my nipples. They were already erect from all of the whorish excitement.

One man jumped up and ran over to me. He sucked on of my nipples into his mouth and ran his arm around me. I reached down and grabbed his cock, but Al jumped up and told him to sit down.

"If we gotta draw lots boys," he said, "we will, otherwise sit and wait 'till I tell ya it's your turn!"

I walked up and kissed Al, whispering to him.

"Thanks sweetheart," I said.

He just squeezed my ass in acknowledgment.

I went back to the boy's strip show. I raised my skirt to show the men my bush. They howled.

I started to run my fingers through my hairy bush, slipping a finger in and pulling it out to show the men that I already had black cum in me. As I pulled my fingers out, globs of cum came out too. I ate it as I talked.

"Do I get any more of this boys?" I asked.

"Oh yeah, baby," Eddie answered, "you're gonna get a lot of it!"

The men started laughing, the beer starting to kick in and the tension in the room starting to drop. I unhooked and unwrapped my skirt and let it drop to the floor. All I had left on were my pearls, stockings, and high heels.

What a sight I was! Here I was, a married white woman standing in stockings and heels in front of nine horny black men, my wet naked cunt open for all to see.

I continued the show. I started to grasp my horny cunt lips with my long, red fingernails. I was getting myself extremely, uncontrollably horny!

Al instructed me to turn around. When I did, the men cheered when the saw my ass. Al came up to me and told me to bend over. I looked at him and bent over, holding him by the waste with my head at his waist. I reached into his robe and turned to look at each man as I fondled Al's cock.

Al reached behind me and spread my ass checks with his hands to expose the asshole he gaped open a short time ago.

"Already opened her ass up for you boys."

I could hear the jokes flying, some of the men throwing things at Al.

Al lifted me up and ran his hand between my legs and up to my cunt. I continued to hold his semi-limp cock in my hand as I spread my legs a little more to let him finger me in front of the men.

"Nice tight pussy, too!"

Al then pulled me close to him. He kissed me, rubbing his hands between my legs. I'm sure the feeling was as powerful for him as it was for me, kissing and being felt up in front of all of these men.

When Al stopped, I sat down on the floor in front of the men. Al looked down at me as I started to unstrap my high heels.

"No, baby," he said, "we're gonna fuck you with your stockings and shoes on."

By now each man was jacking his cock, in anticipation of what they were going to do for me. They were magnificent cocks. The smallest was 8" and the two largest ones were a little bigger than Al! My cocks ranged in shade from light brown to the night black. I loved the different shares of color.

As I sat on the floor, I was getting incredibly excited at the prospect of servicing this much wonderful black cock. Al then stood in front of me so the whole room could see what he was about to do.

His robe was tied shut at the waist. Al didn't bother to untie it. He just pulled open the bottom of his robe, allowing his big black cock to dangle in front my face.

"Suck it, white bitch."

The whorish fuckfest had begun.

Chapter Eleven

I was mesmerized by the live sex show of which I was the center of attention. I have never felt so sexy and desirable as I did when I glanced around to see that pack of horny black studs jerking their cocks, waiting for their turn with me.

I kneeled up in front of Al and sucked his hanging soft cock into my mouth to the sound of cheering men. I sucked Al harder and harder, until the full glory of his huge black meat was again stretching my mouth open.

I pulled the black fuck stick out of my mouth, and placed the great mushroom head on my outstretched tongue. I gazed up at Al as I rotated my tongue around his stiff prick.

Al looked down at me smiled.

"Ahhhh, that's it sweet bitch, suck the cum out of my cock."

While Al enjoyed his second blowjob from "his slut," he started to invite the men to sample my wares. Jimmy was the first to start, the man in his mid-60's.

"Better get over a get a piece of this hot white bitch while she's still fresh, old man," Al said.

Jimmy didn't need any more encouragement. In a flash, he was behind me on his knees. Al sat down in front of me, and

Jimmy just pushed me over to Al's waiting cock. Jimmy started licking my quivering cunt.

"Damn, she's wet!" he commented.

Jimmy licked some more and started fingering my sloppy cunt.

"This is one tight white woman you got here Al," he said.

"That pussy is tighter than a drum," Al responded.

Jimmy didn't eat me out for too long. He kneed up and started to worm his black snake into my cunt lips. The crowd of men starting yelling to Jimmy.

"Stick it to her Jimmy . . . stick it to the horny white bitch."

As Jimmy inched his long cock into my cunt, I sucked Al back into my mouth, trying desperately to get the fat fuck stick into my throat. I was gagging myself, bent on doing so. I pushed the fucker further and further in, getting it about half way in.

Jimmy then started pounding away at my cunt. He fucked me so hard his balls slapped at my ass. He grunted and moaned with each stroke of his black cock through my wet cunt. He was thoroughly enjoying his piece of young, married white ass.

"Ohhhh . . . her pussy sure is hot," he said.

Rubbing my hair, Al looked down at me and asked me a question.

"You like Jimmy giving to you, huh baby?"

"Y . . . e . . . s," I moaned as I slobbered on his fat prick.

Al, the cocksman that he is, isn't so easy at cumming. Apparently realizing that he could fuck my mouth for an hour before blowing, he tugged his tool out of my throat to give his buds a chance.

Al told Fred, the man in his 50's, to come and take his place. As my body was being pushed back and forth by the intensity of Jimmy's thrusts, I watched Fred race on over. A crusty old fucker, I thought.

True to the image I had of him, Fred sat in front of me, held his tool straight up, and put his hand on the back of my head to slam my mouth down on his cock with a violent force.

I could feel Fred's big black cock throb in my mouth as the fucker grabbed me by the ears, forcing his long black fuck stick into my throat until my chin was resting on his balls. He then pulled my head up and down on it.

"Bitch sure can swallow cock, Al," he said gleefully.

"Fucking right," Al shot back, "my bitches get taught how to swallow cock."

I pressed my hands against Fred's legs to brace myself from Jimmy's thrusts and started to work the fuck stock in and out of my throat.

I reveled the feeling of having two men in me at the same time, especially knowing the seven more were watching and waiting for service.

Jimmy couldn't take much, and soon was pumping a load of his seed up my cunt.

"See if this knocks your slut up, Al," Jimmy said as he pounded his load into me.

Al looked at the men and yelled out.

"My bitch better not leave her without a black baby in her, or none of you will ever get another piece of her!"

The comment set the men off. They started hollering and laughing, each one jerking his shaft faster and faster.

As soon as Jimmy dismounted, Bobby, the fat man, ran up to take his place. The rest of men started chanting.

"Knock her up!"

"Knock her up!"

"Knock her up!"

Bobby quickly had his equally fat tool worming into my fertile cunt, intent on complying with Al's wishes. His balls slapped against me getting ready to dump its load.

The incredible spectacle and the growing smell of raw sex in the air caused me to instinctively push myself backwards onto Bobby's hot cock until I was fully stuffed with his black meat.

I kept sucking Fred in and out of my throat as the vile dialogue between Al and his friends continued. I was determined to get some more black seed in my mouth, so I reached down and started rubbing Fred's balls and asshole as I joined the fray.

"Damn, I want a black baby stud," I moaned.

"Oh fuck, splash me with your hot nigger seed!"

Moaning like a bastard, it was no time before Fred was dumped his load into my mouth. I clamped my mouth shut tight around the shaft so none of his cum would be lost.

As my mouth began to fill, I gulped down a huge wad of Fred's thick cum as fast as I could. There was just too much. The wad built up in my mouth faster than I could swallow, and the volume forced it to elude the tight grip of my lips on the cock head and run down my chin.

I pulled the snake out to catch the escaping cum with my fingers as soon as I could, but it had already started to drip onto my tits. As I pulled the cock out, I could feel the growing load starting to pour from my lips. I swallowed as fast as I could, but it was just too heavy a load for my small mouth.

And the fucker's balls weren't empty yet. The fucker kept cumming and cumming in my mouth, moaning like a bull as he held my head in place. I reacted as fast as I could to the dripping cum, but I was new to a man with this much cum.

I pushed Fred's rod deeper in my throat to try to keep from losing any more precious hot cum, but the spurting thick cock still caused some to splash out of my engorged mouth as it went into my throat. Fred's prick then blasted another shot into my throat, the jet hitting the back of my mouth with such force that I felt it on my tonsils. The amount of flowing cum was overwhelming.

I eventually relented, pulling the cock out of my throat until only the spurting head was still in my mouth. The bastard's balls were drained in no time.

When Fred was done shooting his wad, I pushed out my tongue for everyone to see Fred's load on it, and then I swallowed like a hungry whore! Fred saw me and snapped at me.

"You fucking cunt, that was going into your ripe pussy!"

Fred was pissed that he missed a chance to implant me. Too bad fucker, I thought.

I was able to swallow it first! Damn! The sticky salty taste of Fred's wad was incredible.

"Sorry baby," I said sheepishly as I swallowed the last of it, "but I love the taste of Mandingo cum!"

Fred stood up and the next man took his place as I rubbed Fred's cum on my nipples.

"Damn," Fred said as he saw me, "she does love nigger cum!"

Bobby wasn't far behind in dropping a load, clearly a man who couldn't last long when faced with hot pussy and a sex show! His body tensed and he blasted his load in to mix with Jimmy's.

The slopping sound from Bobby's grinding his load into my dripping cunt was loud enough for anyone close to hear. It was amazing. As Bobby shot his load, he grunted to me.

"Take my nigger seed, white bitch. Take it up your tight little cunt."

I could hear Al in the background yelling.

"Fucking right!"

Both men then dismounted from my ravished holes, and I looked up to see who would be replacing them. Dave, the stud about my age, came over and laid down on his back.

Sensing what Dave wanted, I climbed over his body and reached down to grab his long fuck stick. I jacked it a few times with my hand to make sure that it was good and hard. I slowly inched my cunt down on him.

When Dave's black prick was halfway in, I swiftly impaled myself on his mammoth pole in one fast stroke. It caused us both to moan in whorish ecstasy. I could feel Dave's big tool push the cum out of my cunt as it slipped deep inside me. It was an unbelievably decadent feeling.

Dave then reached behind me and grabbed my ass, forcing my head down. He used my ass cheeks as leverage to lift and slam my cunt down on his hard cock. God, this was great.

I helped Dave by bouncing my cunt up and down on his shaft, my tits swaying in front of his face. He would occasionally reach up to suck on my swelling nipples, and even kissed my cum-breath mouth once.

Dave did me like that for a few minutes, and then he flipped me over on my back with one muscular move.

Once on my back, Dave lifted my legs so my ankles were up by my neck, and he proceeded to pound me with his great black cock.

I rubbed Dave's smooth black ass as he pounded away on my cunt. Every now and then he stopped pounding me to look down at my face.

"You want me to cum in your pussy, baby?"

I moaned loudly in response each time he asked me the question. I then looked him in the eye and told him what he wanted to hear.

"Please splash my ripe little eggs with your hot seed!"

It aroused the horny fucker beyond belief. A few long, hard strokes later, and the bastard started to grunt. Dave's back stiffened, and the bastard buried his cock deep into my cunt. With the cock firmly embedded between my legs, the stud emptied his balls.

After Dave got off from me, I told them that my legs were getting numb. Al called to have a small kitchen table brought out, and in no less than a minute it was in the middle of the living room! He took me by my hand and gently guided me to it.

Al placed me so I was standing facing the table, and then he pushed me down so my elbows were on it. It wasn't very wide.

"That's it, baby," he said, "bend over and it'll make it easier for you."

I knew it would only be a second before I was impaled with another hard black cock. Sure enough, Eddie walked up behind me and placed his hand on the middle of my back. He pushed my face down onto the table.

"Spread your legs, cunt," he commanded as he kicked one of my legs over.

I spread my legs about three feet apart, making sure I could still stand. I focused intently on what was going to happen, so I only barely heard the front door open. More black men came in to the room. Oh my God!!!

Al invited his new friends in and told them to be sure to knock up my ripe white cunt. I wondered how much black cock my delicate little body could withstand.

Eddie was an especially brutal mother fucker, with a cock that had to be size of Al's from the feel of the throbbing head being pushed into from behind. I was pretty slicked up by that point, so the bastard wasn't able to do much damage. Eddie just slipped his cock into the gooey channel, forcing more left over cum to spurt out.

"Christ, man, she's fucking wet," he said, as he began to stroke my cunt.

"At least that ass is still nice and dry!"

I knew it was only a matter of time before I would have a big black bone stuck in my ass. I didn't realize until now that Eddie would be the dirty bastard to do it.

After giving me about five deep strokes with his black cock, Eddie started to get pissed at the fact that my cunt wasn't as tight as it was for the first men.

"Al, can I fuck your slut in the ass?" Eddie asked.

"Absolutely, my man," Al replied, "you can fuck her ass 'till the bitch can't sit!"

There it was.

Eddie was quick to take his piece of my asshole, replying to Al.

"Fine. I'll take your white bitch's ass."

I had come to find that the ass fucks were too much for me to handle . . . it was the one sex act that truly sent me over the edge. I lifted my ass for Eddie to take it.

Eddie pulled his cock from my sloppy cunt, and pushed the head against my puckered asshole. I could feel my ass flower quiver as the big head pushed against it.

The black bastard was ruthless. He gripped my ass firmly so he could hold me in place as he popped my ass. He started grunting as the cock head made its way in past the tight anal ring.

Eddie wasn't having an easy time of it. My asshole must have tightened since Al opened it, I though. As the fucker worked his blast monster into my tight ass, I clutched the sides of the tables and started to moan and grunt.

My legs trembled from the feeling of what Eddie's stiff prick was doing to me, a fact he obviously enjoyed.

"That's it, baby, take Eddie's big black cock up your tight white ass!"

The words rang in my ears, and I moaned loudly to let him know I had no objections. When his big black prick finally slammed rock bottom, the sensation caused my mouth to pop open.

The black bastard began to deep fuck my ass. I clutched the sides of the table harder and my head swooned, again instinctively thrashing around. My ass was taking quite a long dicking. The site was too much for the men, and lines started forming behind Eddie and in front of my face.

A dark-skinned stud came and stood in front of my face. This total stranger could see that I was getting my ass fucked too hard to slip his cock into my mouth. He must have been afraid that I would bite it off. So he stood there jacking his black cock.

"Ohhh, baby, Eddie's really popping your ass," he said.

I moaned in response, causing Eddie to tell me as it was.

"That's right, bitch, Eddie's gonna pump his nigger seed into your sweet little ass!"

The man in front of me was quite excited.

"I ain't never seen a white the bitch who loves cock so much," he said.

"Goddamn Al, where you get this one?"

The man then pointed his big cock up at my head, which was facing down looking at the floor. I looked up. The bastard started to blow, blasting thick streams of cum onto my face.

The hot cum splashed my forehead and lips, and I desperately tried to catch it with my tongue. My hands were too busy grasping the table so I could keep standing while my ass was fucked. Gravity worked against me for most of the load, though, and it just dripped off my face onto the floor. That actually made me sad.

Eddie was still taking my ass, no end in sight. What a fucking stud! I started to relax a bit, just standing there taking the pounding.

These depraved black fuckers sure were relishing the opportunity to have a married white woman! The next man came up and took the stranger's place in front of me.

The next man in line just walked up a jammed his cock into my mouth. I sucked wildly, sucking in as much as I could. It was hard given how Eddie was ass fucking me. Seeing that I was too pinned by Eddie to deep throat him, the bastard placed his hand on the back of my head and used it as leveraged to work his cock into my throat.

"Ahhhh," he said, reaching to grab my head with both of his hands.

The black stranger fucked proceeded to fuck my throat like it was a cunt. He took long deep strokes, working his cock in and out of my mouth as he held my head.

As the stud neared climax, he took a little more liberty with me, starting to work his cock in and out of my throat faster and faster until he imbedded his cock into me and popped his load.

I sucked and swallowed the cum from this man's balls, and when he started to pull out I sucked harder hoping he wouldn't leave.

"Let go of my cock, you fucking cunt," he said, yanking his cock out.

"Fuck me dude," he said to Al, "this is one cock-starved white bitch."

As the next man approached me, Eddie was finally getting ready to cum.

"Get ready, baby, here it comes," he said.

Eddie pounded my ass harder than he had before, making sure he shot as much cum as he could. He slammed the big fuck stick in one last time, blasting scalding hot spunk into my bowels.

"Take it all, bitch, take it all," he said as he held my ass close to his groin.

Eddie then pumped my ass with his shaft a few more time, stroking the last of his cum into my ass. He held his prick there, my tight ass forcing it out as it softened.

I now had a new stranger in front of me, a very tall man. He was one of the new guys who just came over. The man was kind of weird. He apparently liked hair, as he wrapped his cock in my long hair and began jack himself off with my hair.

I tried to suck the man, but I could only occasionally get the hair-covered cockhead into my mouth. It was so frustrating.

As this went on, the next man in the train slipped his hot cock into my cunt. As I tried to push back on the new cock behind me, the man in front continued to jack off.

The stud in front finally started to cum. I could feel thick globs of seed shooting throughout my hair. This fucker must have pumped a half gallon of cum into my hair, causing Al to yell out.

"Man, you're a sick fucker," Al said, as he took out a camera and started taking snapshots.

I was so horny and driven by lust, I didn't care. I just took the next man in my mouth.

The man behind me stroked me long and hard for a few minutes, and it wasn't long before he came inside my pussy. He, too, was then replaced by another of the new entries.

The next man simply walked up behind me, unzipped his pants nonchalantly, and swiftly slammed his big black bone all the way up my cunt. I could feel the other men's seed slosh out of me when he did it. I wondered if he loved it as much as I did.

The new fucker behind me stroked my sloppy cunt fast and deep, holding my hips for leverage. With each stroke, I could feel the material of his pants hitting my ass cheeks. It was an incredible experience being bent over a table, wearing stocking and with my high heels still on, a total stranger I have never seen just whipping out his black cock and taking me with his pants still on.

I could hear the strangers voice.

"You said this white bitch is married?"

A few of the men answered him that it was true, and the bastard reached over a whispered in my ear.

"Does your husband know how bad you crave black cock, baby?"

Infuriated at the comment, I stopped sucking the man in front of me long enough to respond.

"Fuck you asshole."

That pissed off the black stranger behind me. He started banging my cunt with as much force as he could muster, slapping my ass as he did so.

"Fucking white cunt, fuck you. I'll teach your cunt a lesson. You're old man will never feel the sides of your trashy cunt."

Al walked over, apparently sensing that there might be trouble.

"Take it easy Joey," he said.

"Fucking white bitch," the man replied.

Joey, I guess his name was, pounded me harder and harder, and then started to have another idea. He quickly withdrew his cock, and immediately jammed it in my ass.

"Your asshole, too, cunt," he said.

"I'm going to find your fucking husband and tell him Joey and the boys reamed it out."

What a dickhead, I thought. But the punishment this asshole thought he was giving me only excited me more, bringing my cock sucking skills to a new height. I sucked off the man in front of me and then took another as quickly as I could.

Joey, the asshole behind me, banged me for a few more minutes and shot his load. Not much of a stud, I thought.

"Here you go, you fucking whore, tell hubby Joey blasted a thick wad of nigger spunk up your ass!"

I stopped sucking to shoot back a remark to the jerk.

"Rip my asshole open then, you fucking asshole, if you think you can."

But he was spent. He couldn't. At least not now.

"I'll be back for your ass, white bitch," he said.

The next man in line had heard my offer.

"I'll rip your ass open for you baby," he said, "no problem."

My asshole was long-dicked again. When the man came, my backside was quickly replaced by another hot cock. This fucker slammed his rod deep into my ass in one fell swoop without any warning. I let out a sluttish moan, and the fucker came in less than a minute.

The next man took his place, slipping his prick into my drenched pussy. My body was on fire from all of these hot black cocks! I yelled out.

"I'm a whore, a white fucking whore," I cried, "fuck me with those huge big black cocks!"

That was the new stud's cue to start working my cunt over. In a matter of seconds, another bastard was in front of me. He grabbed me by the hair and lifted my head with it. He held out his black cock in his other hand, and dropped my open mouth on his cock.

I waited for a second to savor the feel of the hot cock as it throbbed in my mouth I sucked hungrily on the new hot cock, waiting for its load of tasty scum. It didn't take long.

It was no time at all before these men turned me into a voracious cocksucker, entranced by the taste and feel of wads of hot sticky cum. I needed more cum.

I reached around the man I was blowing, I grabbed his ass cheeks and pulled him further into my mouth, enticing the bastard to fuck my mouth like a cunt. My lips quivered as the fucker took my mouth, and my legs began to tremble as the fucker behind me slammed his cock deep up my cunt over and over.

Excited by the passion of getting banged from both ends, I braced myself and raised my ass so the man behind me could work his fuck stick into my cunt as deep as possible.

My whorish performance was too much for them, and in no time they both erupted their hot scum into my convulsing holes. By that time, I could feel the long strings of hot black cum running down my thighs and stockings. It was so hot as it slid down my skin. It was so decadent, I loved it.

The man in front of me was quickly replaced, the man behind savoring the feel of my cunt squeezing shut on his softening prick. Using my mouth like it was a cunt, the new man worked his cock down my throat like a pro.

I enjoyed the sweet feeling of servicing the new black cock, rubbing the set of balls that were dangling right in front of my face as my throat was stuffed deep with the huge cock that operated them.

"Ahhhh!!!!!!!!!!" he exclaimed, "lick my balls."

I immediately complied, lifting the huge fuck stick and licking all over his hairy sac.

While I serviced the man in front, I was ass fucked, a new man coming up behind me and spearing me with his hot black cock. I clinched my asshole shut on his cock to increase the pleasure for both of us, causing him to grip my waist and rip the cock from my eager hole. I think it was at that point that I truly became used to having a man's pole up my ass.

I then deep throated the fucker in front of me, pulling him into my throat by wrapping my hands around to his tight ass cheeks. Once I had myself firmly impaled on the stud's hot prick, he succumbed to the temptation like this friends before him. He grabbed me by the ears and brutally mouth fucked me.

Seeing my hands free, two men came on either side of me and unzipped their pants. They whipped out two stiff black cocks and placed the hot peckers in the palms of my hands. I ran my soft white fingers up and down the throbbing shafts and over the soft cock heads, savoring the feel of their hot sticks.

My mouth was getting fucked and my ass was getting slammed. I wanted more. I squeezed my hand around cocks on my sides and started to jack them off to the rhythm of my ass fucking and deep throating.

The men getting jerked off took soon over and started rubbing their hot pricks across my back as they jerked themselves off. They both started to moan as they gave me a hot bath with their thick, sticky seed.

The decadent sight caused the man behind me to join in, withdrawing his slick pole from my asshole to shoot a thick jet of hot scum that spunked up my ass cheeks and onto my back.

The man in front was also overwhelmed by the whorish spectacle, wrenching his cock from my throat to jerk his cock off onto my face. The black bastard dosed my face with such a load of cum that the globs just dripped off my face to the floor, much like a leaking ceiling.

My body was literally drench with gobs of black jizz. My god, I loved being the center of such a decadent, whorish scene with all of these black men!

Chapter Twelve

Man after man came and fucked me. They used my pussy, my ass, my throat, my hands, and even my hair to service their horny pricks. I lost count, but I think I had drained about 25 black cocks.

As I started to count how many men enjoyed me, I looked around and realized that all but two people used me. One was the quiet stranger in the corner, Alvin. The other was the young boy, Nick. He stood around just stroking his dick. He was clearly too shy to join in the spectacle he was watching.

Nick's cock wasn't a bad piece of meat for someone so young. I'd say he sported a good 8" cock. It wasn't very thick, but it was still thicker than my husbands.

Once the other men were done using me, they started taunting Nick.

"Hey boy!" Eddie said, "come fuck this bitch!"

Eddy was the one who so violently reamed out my ass, the first of the men to do it to me that night. Eddie struck me as a truly mean man, someone who used women and degraded them at every opportunity. Nick just shook his head no.

"You little pussy!" Eddie said again, " you momma aint' taught you to fuck?"

Nick was really a shy kid. I started to realize that he had to be a virgin. Here he was in this debauchery, this spectacle of lust, and all he could do was stroke his rigid pole.

I thought Eddie was being unnecessarily hateful to this young kid. Then something happened that startled me. Eddie demanded that I take the role of teacher as the man behind me climaxed and withdrew.

"Hey bitch, get the little bastard between your legs!" he ordered.

I didn't want to force this young boy to do anything he didn't want to do, especially something like sex that would influence the rest of his life. As drunk and in heat as I was, I refused.

"Leave the kid alone!" I said.

That really pissed Eddie off. He came over to me and raised his hands.

"Fuck you bitch," he said, "you'll do as you're told."

I thought he was going to start beating me, and I was terrified. At that moment, Al came up and caught the fist as it was coming down on me.

"Get out of my house," he said calmly, "you ain't hurtin' my lady."

At that moment, my feelings for Al completely changed. Yes, Al was a brutal cocksman, but he showed compassion and a sense of loyalty to me. I respected that he was defending me.

Eddie got really pissed when Al said that, yelling at Al.

"You're lady? She ain't no fuckin' lady," he said. "She's a fuckin' white gutter whore!"

That really upset Al, and he took a swing at Eddie. They started fighting, and then Alvin came out of the corner and grabbed Eddie. Eddie was clearly drunk, but they weren't going to let him hurt me. Damn! Al wasn't even going to let him insult me!

A fight started to break out, and six of the naked men forced Eddie out the door. I was happy to see him thrown out.

Once Eddie was gone, Alvin went back to his corner and sipped his beer. Al came up to me and rubbed my stomach.

"It's ok baby, nobody's gonna hurt you," he said softly.

I looked up at Al and whispered to him.

"Thank you!"

I was truly amazed. That incident changed my attitude about that whole night, and it made me understand that what these men were saying and doing was all in good fun. When one of them crossed the line, the others stopped it. As strange as it may sound, I felt safe and secure in this room full of horny black men.

Al then made a comment to me about Nick.

"If the kid don't wanna fuck you, don't force him," he said, "Eddie's just an asshole."

Nick looked down, like he was kind of ashamed. He was so adorable standing there with that innocent look to him. I stood up and called him over to me.

"Nickie," I said, "come here and talked to me."

Nick walked over in a sheepish manner.

I slowly reached out and gently took his cock in my hand when he got close to me. I started to jerk it softly.

"It's ok if you don't want to fuck me Nickie."

"I wanna fuck you ma'am," he said, "but I don't know if I can with these guys watching me."

I walked up to Al and whispered to him.

"Can we use your bedroom Al?" I asked.

"Good ahead baby," he said, "but be gentle with my boy!"

"It's upstairs on the left," he added.

I took Nick by the cock and pulled him up the stairs. Once we were in the bedroom. I turned around and shut the door. I then stood close to him and wrapped my arms around him.

"We're all alone, Nickie," I said as I kissed his shoulders and chest.

"I'm 36 Nickie, how old are you," I asked.

"18 ma'am," he said.

"You ever been with a white woman," I asked?

I didn't know if it were true or not, but I didn't care. I wanted to help this young boy enjoy some of the new sexual adventures that so completely changed my own life that day.

"No ma'am, I actually ain't never been with a woman," he said bashfully, "but please don't tell the others."

A virgin!

A black buck virgin!

I wanted to help this boy so much. Damn! I wanted to FUCK him! All the white women this young stud would fuck in his life, and I was destined to be his first!

I never thought of myself as a cougar. Hell, I go to church every week and had never been with anyone but my husband. For some reason, after all that had happened to me, I thought it was destiny that I was to deflower this cute black boy.

I reached down and stroked Nickie's cock some more. He leaned down and kissed me as he slid his hand between my legs. I spread a bot to encourage him.

Nickie and I kissed for a few moments as he felt me up. Then I felt his soft muscular hands come around and start rubbing my ass. He had me hot at this point, and his hand on my ass sent me over the edge.

"Nickie, you wanna fuck me?"

"God yes, I do," he said.

I took his hand and led him to the bed. I climbed on and arranged the pillows so they would be under my neck. I raised my legs and spread wide. I started to finger my cunt.

"Nickie, please put that beautiful cock between my legs," I moaned.

Nick came up and kneeled down between my legs. He held his cock, unsure of himself. I took the cock and gently pulled him until the head was at my gash. I reached around to his firm ass and pulled him to me. The cock started to slide into my cum-lubbed pussy. He then collapsed on me and started to stroke his cock.

I fucked Nick back with everything I had. I wanted to make his first experience something he would never forget. Remembering how much Bill and Al's filthy talk inflamed me, I decided to throw gasoline onto this boy's fire.

"Oh God, Nickie," I cried, "your cock is so big!"

Nick grunted and pushed.

I grabbed Nick's head and brought his lips to mine. I ran my tongue furiously against his, pushing my hips to meet his every thrust.

"Please fuck me," I cried, "stroke that big cock off between my legs!"

I wrapped my legs around his back and let him use my pussy.

"God, cum in me, please, I want to feel your cum," I moaned.

Nick had been fucking me about 3 minutes or so. But the first feel of pussy was too much for him. I felt his back stiffen and he slammed his balls against my ass. He shot his wad deep into me, grunting like a dog.

Once Nick had cum, he collapsed on me. I kissed his neck and whispered in his ear.

"You're going to be a great black stud," I told him.

"Thank you ma'am," he politely said.

I kissed his ear and whispered again.

"White women will go crazy over you if you treat 'em good!"

"I will ma'am," he said.

Nick then rolled off from me, and I bent down between his legs. I took his limp dick into my mouth and sucked the cum off from it. What the hell, I thought. I loved the taste of cum.

Once I finished, I got up and went into Al's bathroom. I need a little relief! I saw a robe Al had, and I put it on. I combed my hair.

"Tell Al I'll be out in a sec," I said.

Chapter Thirteen

I went back downstairs to find that many of the men had left. Al came up to me and gave me a deep kiss, and then he handed me a beer.

I took a few drinks and walked over to the sofa to sit down. I needed a rest.

While I was tired and sore from the way I was being used as a fuck toy by the pack of horny black men, at that point I didn't think that there was anything these guys could do to me that I couldn't take. It was then that the only man in the original group who hadn't had me, or even stripped, walked up and stood before me.

Alvin yelled to Al.

"Goddamn, man, when do I get to fuck her?"

I found out later that Al had told Alvin that he couldn't fuck me until Al told him it was ok. Now, it was ok.

"Ok man, go ahead and enjoy my woman," Al said.

"Finally!" Alvin responded.

I could only wonder what the hell that all meant. Why did he have to wait? Oh, who cares, I thought. What's one more fuck?

Little did I realize that this was going to be the absolute fuck of my entire life.

Alvin took my hand and helped me off from the couch. He took me in his arms and kissed me. I kissed Alvin back passionately, reaching down between his legs as he reached in front of me and pushed his fingers into my sopping when slit.

Alvin's cock was still limp, but even limp and through his pants it struck me as fairly big. A nice big cock, I thought!

Alvin continued to kiss me as he danced me back to the kitchen table. He then looked at the group of men standing around me and gave instructions to his friends.

"Ok, guys, flip her up on the table on her back," he said.

I was startled. What the hell's going on, I thought. Before I could say anything, four naked men came up to me and grabbed me by my arms and legs. They swiftly hoisted me up and landed me flat on my back on the middle of the table.

Alvin stood in front of me and started to get undressed. I leaned up on my elbows to see what all of commotion was about.

"Baby, this is your lucky night," Alvin said as he took off his shirt.

"You're gonna know what it feels like to really get fucked!"

When Alvin was down to his shorts, I could see what was about to happen. The bulge in his crotch looked like a fucking third leg. As Alvin slipped off his shorts, I was literally paralyzed by the sight before me. This gorgeous buck nigger had a cock that defied imagination.

Alvin was truly a freak of nature, his deformed cock hanging down to his knees. The beastly thing had to be at least 16" in length as he picked it up and started stroking it in front of me.

Alvin looked like a man working with a boa constrictor. The mushroom shaped cock head was wider than a large peach. His balls hung down, dangling between his legs.

I was mesmerized like never before during this whorish day. The bastard couldn't even get HIS hand around the shaft, the fucker was so thick! How could it possibly fit inside my cunt?

Al came up to me and told me that they call him The Impaler, and that they never let him fuck anything until they've all had a turn because he ruins it for them.

"Oh, shit," I thought.

Out of panic, I started to move, turning to get up and end this.

Seeing this, Al came up behind my head wrapped his strong arms around my upper chest. Cupping one of my tits in his hands, he kissed my cum soaked lips.

"You're doing great baby," he said softly, "you take Alvin here, and you can be my bitch."

I started to protest, my eyes bulging out of my head as the pole got hard. Al tried to sooth me by reminding me that he hadn't let me down yet. His words didn't matter much to me at that point, but his arms were strong enough to keep my already weak body down.

It didn't take Alvin long to have that slab of cock meat as hard as cold steel. He proudly walked over to me, ready for his piece of white ass.

"Spread your legs, baby," he said calmly.

I was immobilized looking at that humongous cock. I couldn't take my eyes off from it. Alvin sensed from my wide eyes that he needed a little help.

"The white bitch is freakin' out . . . hold her legs apart."

Two men came up on either side of me and grabbed my legs. They yanked them apart as wide as they possibly could, holding them straight out by my heels and resting them on their shoulder. Alvin walked between my widely spread legs, reaching his hand out to rub my nervous cunt.

My panic increased as Alvin moved inside my spread legs, ready to mount me with his horse cock. My smooth white skin looked incredible with the black buck between my legs, the log in his hand.

I started making unintelligible sounds as Alvin drew closer and closer with his monster cock in his hand, clearly intent on feeding it my little white pussy.

"It's OK, baby, lots of women have enjoyed the Impaler."

Alvin held my slick pussy lips open with one hand. He then guided his telephone pole to my open cunt with his other hand. The tremendous cock head was pushed into my hairy, cum-matted bush. The grease of all the men before him made his task a little easier, but it was still incredibly tight given the enormous size of the cock head.

Applying enough pressure, the throbbing mushroom head eventually split my pussy lips wide open, and the head thrust its way into me. My mouth dropped open as my pussy spasmed at the first assault, tightly gripping the invading monster.

A few inches of the thick shaft followed closely behind it with a thunderous push of Alvin's muscular hips. I really didn't think that I could take this massive fuck stick in my hole, no matter how much the boys had greased me up with their cum. It was fucking gargantuan, monstrous. This is one man who should have been a porno star!

What I thought didn't matter to Alvin. He kept working the huge snake into me, prying my cunt apart as the huge swollen prick rolled into me, the whole against my protests.

"Ah fuck, you bastard," I cried, "it's too big!"

He pushed more.

"Please, oh God!" I cried, "I . . . can't . . . take . . . it!!!"

He pushed more, my pleas only inflaming his passions.

"You fucker!" I cried, "you fucking goddamned nigger!"

Alvin was taking me, and there was nothing I could do to stop him. Al kept my back pinned down, and Alvin's friends held my legs wide apart.

The monstrous prick continued to split my cunt wider than any of these studs had ever hoped to do. I instinctively squirmed my hips up to get the fucker away from me, and I briefly succeeded in getting all but the swollen cock head out of me.

Seeing me pull away from the Impaler, Al held me down tighter, allowing Alvin take me without resistance. Alvin was quick to comment.

"Can't pull away from me, baby," he said coldly.

"I'm gonna open that tight cunt so much your husband will never feel its walls again!"

Here I was on my back, stocking and high heels still on, pinned down and getting laid by some black man's monster cock. Alvin was opening my cunt up like I never dreamed imaginable.

There was no question about it.

I was truly laid.

And I mean LAID.

Not realizing at the moment that a cunt is a resilient creature of nature that can hug any cock, like it can handle the birth of a baby, my mind ran thinking about Mark and Alvin's comment. This black bastard was robbing Mark of something he married. Would Mark ever be able to enjoy me again?

I cried out.

"God, please, no. I'm married! You'll ruin my cunt."

The asshole Joey was quick to respond for Alvin.

"Fuck your husband, you cock hungry bitch!" he said.

"Alvin, my man, make sure her husband can get his arm up that nasty cunt!" he joked.

It helped to solidify Alvin's resolution to ruin my cunt. The black stud -- and I mean STUD -- pushed the monster prick further between my legs, and I grit my teeth I could feel the deep insides of my cunt being spread apart as the massive cock head ground its way further and further into me, causing me to let out a series of whining, sluttish groans.

The cock head soon banged against something deep inside of me, and I swear I could feel what ever it was being pushed apart. The massive cock head just continued to steamroll into my cunt. By the time the fucker had reached rock bottom, I could swear the Mandingo stud had cracked open my uterus and was now probing it with that massive cock head.

I could feel my upright spread legs start to tremble and convulse. I was orgasming! The big buck nigger stud had be cumming all over that formidable cock of his!

Alvin succeeded in getting his giant black dong fully sheathed by my married white cunt, a pleasure that had only been known to my husband when I woke up that morning.

Once Alvin finally had his big dick all the way in me, there was no doubt this fucker had penetrated my fertile womb with his unbelievable cock head. Here I was flat on my back, getting thoroughly laid by this monstrous black cock.

Alvin started to work his cock in and out, slowly and only a few inches at a time. The man was constantly into me up to his balls, the sheer size of the tool forcing cum to splash out of my cunt and onto the table. I never felt so impaled before in my life.

Alvin stroked me more and more, my surely being remolded to accept only the largest of cocks. The feel of the huge snake firmly lodged in my so deep in my cunt along with the slow striking motions caused me to shudder again from a violent orgasm. Alvin had me in heaven in no time, swooning like a well-oiled whore.

I looked down between my legs. I was surprised that my pulverized cunt opened to accept the whole whang on this deformed black bastard. Alvin then braced himself and started to fuck me like I had never been fucked up to that point.

The godlike black stud withdrew his dick slowly, my cunt having tightly snapped onto it. Once he was able to withdraw the fucking monster, he pounded it back in. My cunt fully retracted each time he pulled it out, and split open as he slammed back in, drawing a deep, sluttish groan from my soul.

My cunt was truly taking a beating, being vanquished by this huge black bastard. Each stroke affirmed my womanhood, the bastard truly fucking my womb.

Alvin then pushed off the men holding my legs up. He wrapped his big black arms around my legs so he could get leverage. The bastard then picked up his tempo, and soon his tool was slamming my cunt faster and harder. My cock-stuffed cunt convulsed from the beating of the Impaler's beastly prick.

Alvin was driving me insane with the incredible sensation of lying there, getting thoroughly laid by such a manly stud. And the show was just getting started.

Al finally let go of me so he could watch the spectacle. When he did, my tits began to sway madly from the horrendous fucking Alvin's enormous black cock was giving to me. I started cumming uncontrollably. I could feel my legs literally shake and convulse from the waves of orgasms this monster prick was causing.

Each stroke into the depths of my womanhood opened me, allowing me to feel the hard black cock thrust so deep into me. I tried to watch the fucker pound in and out of me, but the orgasms began to overwhelm my thoughts and cause me to thrash my swooning head in ecstasy.

I was getting hooked on the colossal fucker! Alvin soon had me affirming his belief that I would enjoy his tool.

"Like it now, bitch?" he asked coldly.

"Ahhh, I . . . I'm . . . I'm cumming!" I moaned.

"Enjoy it bitch!" he said as he continued to ride me.

"Ahhh, God, I'm . . . cumming," I said over and over.

The fucking was too much. I never orgasmed so many times in my life. Alvin was truly a stud, and I was his breeding bitch. My lusty emotions overcame my sensibilities.

"I'm almost done, baby," he said teasingly.

No!

I was just getting into it!

How could he stop?

"No, please, a little more, please," I begged.

"Oh, you want it now, huh baby?" he asked.

"Yes, please, stroke . . . me . . . a . . . little . . . more," I moaned.

"Beg bitch!" he demanded, "beg your nigger stud to fuck you!"

I needed his cock. None of these men did to me what he did. I desperately needed that giant cock. I didn't want the orgasms to ever stop! So I begged him like a whore as he commanded.

"Slam my cunt deep . . . Ohhhh . . . don't stop you black bastard," I screamed.

Alvin pounded me for at least twenty more incredible minutes, each second burning into my mind as one of the most wonderful moments in my life. I never knew sex could feel like this! And Alvin. The bastard teased me the whole time.

"Keep begging bitch," he said coldly.

"Tell me what a black cock slut you are and I'll keep riding your slick cunt all night long!"

I begged and begged and begged.

"Please, please, fuck me," I moaned.

"I love your long, thick nigger cock."

I couldn't shut up. Every word I learned that day came spewing out. I was screaming.

"Oh God, I'm a slut!"

"Ohhh, please, nigger-fuck me!"

"I'm a fucking horny slut for your big black cock!!!!"

"Ride me you stud! Ream my cunt with that huge black prick!" I cried.

Alvin kept his word. As long as I proclaimed myself a black cock-loving slut, he gave me more and more of a pounding with that big hot dick.

But all good things must come to an end, or get better. This one was about to get better . . . but not before pure terror flooded my soul.

As Alvin slammed my cunt, I heard Al remind him.

"Make sure you save some of the Impaler for her ass, man, we have to get her hooked."

Again, the fever I was experiencing from the deep fucking didn't allow me to immediately catch the import of the statement. But Alvin heard it. He stopped and withdrew his cock.

Reality came back to me when he didn't slip it back in, instead using his big hands to push my legs in the air. Once my ankles were next to my head, Alvin placed his massive cock head against my pink asshole.

"Well, she's still gapped, dude," he said to Al.

Oh my God! What was happening!

"Oh fuck, no," I cried!

They just ignored me.

Alvin pushed himself into me, and the giant cock head started to enter my quivering asshole. The size of this cock head was truly too much, and I jerked away from it suddenly.

"Hold this bitch down again," he said.

Two naked black men grabbed my shoulders and pinned me to the table. A third

I started to sobbed as he took me, the mascara running down my cum-soaked face..

"Gotta do it baby. You'll thank me later!"

Joey was quick to defend him.

"How you feel now, you fucking cunt?"

Joey came up to me and smacked his stiff pecker on my face.

"Yeah man! Open this white bitch's ass. Split her right down the middle!" he said as he started to jerk his cock.

I tried to squirm away from Alvin some more, but the men holding me down made it impossible.

Joey, seeing my desire to pull away, bent down by my ear and added another parting shot.

"You fucking horny cunt, now your old man will know your nice white ass has been open for business! Long, thick, hard BLACK business!"

Joey then blasted a load on my lips. As much as I love cum, I couldn't open my mouth as I gritted my teeth from the brutal anal invasion. The wad just stayed on my red lipsticked lips.

This whole spectacle aroused Alvin more. Once he had about 5 inches of his cock into my ass from pushing, he acted to counter my squirming. The black beast grabbed my waist with both of his hands and literally pulled my asshole onto his immense black shaft. He got at least 6 more inches in that way.

I thought I was being split in two, and it caused me to grit my teeth harder and grip the sides of the table as tight as I could. The horny black men never missed an opportunity to get off.

A crowd had formed around the table to watch the horse show. The sight of Alvin taking my ass and Joey's cum on my lips was too much for them.

Two of the horny black fuckers jumped up and pushed Joey aside. They proceeded to paint my lips with a huge amount of thick, gooey cum. By now my mouth was slowly opening from the ass fucking and the smell of all that cum. My tongue rolled out, licking the cum from my lips.

Man after man then started coming up to me and jerking off on my face as Alvin kept working more and more of his horse cock into my ass. The new feelings of deep lust compelled me to start blurting out again.

"Ahhhhh . . . fuck!" I swooned.

My asshole opened much like my cunt had, spreading before the heavy leviathan it was being pulled onto. My squeals started to grow louder and more rapid, enticing the black stud to have my ass.

By now Alvin had about 10 inches of rock hard black cock up my ass. Not good enough. He wanted all of it in.

Alvin then suddenly withdrew about 6 inches of his massive prick, and quickly slammed it right back in again. That got him another inch of impalement.

"Ahhhh . . . fuck," I moaned again as I started to rub all of the cum around my face.

Another black man jumped on the opportunity to fill my body with hot seed. He walked up and started unloading on my nipples. I reached down and massaged the hot seed all over my swollen tits.

Alvin then proceeded to ream me out. He withdrew and slammed his long, hard snake into over and ever, each time working a little more of the tool into me. Eventually, Alvin had me totally impaled on the monstrous cock. My ass canal was fully stuffed by a foot and a half of hard black cock.

For a while after Alvin finally took me, I couldn't move. I was paralyzed by the feeling of the huge monster cock stuck deep into my guts. This bastard had cracked my ass open unlike Bill or Al before him.

Having ripped his way in, Alvin then began to drill my ass with his mammoth black cock, first with slow short strokes, and then with long hard ones. Each time Alvin stroked my ass he drew a squeal from my mouth.

Alvin slammed the whole fucking thing in and out of my ass, stroking my ass by pulling his snake out all the way before he would ram in back in, for a solid 10 minutes.

Damn, I thought! This fucker's been pounding my body for almost an hour!

Alvin kept going. Each stroke caused me to moan. Over and over, I moaned an incredibly whorish "Ahhhhhhhhhh . . . Fuck" to the crowd.

The ass boning continued, arousing me to a new level of lust and passion. My head was soon swooning and thrashing even more, non-stop whorish moans uncontrollably escaping from my soul.

"Ahhhh . . ."

The sight of seeing me getting into this brutal ass fucking caused the men holding me down to back off. They, too, had to be excited, as they started to jack their cocks as my swooning head swayed to each side. Each time my head turned in their direction, they would slap their hard black cocks on my cheek.

My tits swayed from the pounding my asshole was taking. Two men came up and started violently squeezing them, bringing me to new heights of passion. My head thrashed harder as Alvin took my ass, the whorish moans growing louder and louder.

I was cumming.

I couldn't stop cumming.

"Ahhhhhhhhhh . . . Fuck . . .!"

"Ahhhhhhhhhh . . . Fuck . . .!"

"Ahhhhhhhhhh . . . Fuck . . .!"

Two more men came in front of me as I groaned. They were soon blasting chunks of hot black scum all over my face and hair.

The men were soon replaced by other studs who continued to rub their hot black cocks over my tits, taking every opportunity to spunk up my face and chest.

Alvin didn't stop reaming out my ass with his monstrous cock. He continued to long dick my asshole with no end in sight as man after man walked up to me and shot their sticky wads on my face and tits.

As Alvin tore through my asshole, my forehead and chin becoming caked in cum from all of the black bastards excited by the spectacle. I was becoming drunk by sex, the hot man seed splashing my body.

More strange black men started to come in and surround me, a fact I could barely discern. It seemed that Al was going to let the entire hood come by to help implant the married white lady.

Al was not as protective of his new find as I thought he would be. Any black man with a cock could stick it in me and cum. I couldn't keep count. He told me the next day he stopped counting at 60.

Even the great stud Alvin couldn't last forever. I heard him start grunting like an animal for the first time. He grabbed my waist tighter. He was close. Alvin slammed me as hard as he ever had a few times and then he stopped, his unreal fuck stick buried deep in my guts. He let lose a torrential flood of cum.

Damn, what a feeling. Alvin's cock felt like a fucking fire hose going off in my ass. As he painted my bowels with the hot seed the flowed from his humongous cock, he remarked.

"Man, what a hot ass."

When Alvin finished, I was all but wiped out. I was exhausted. But men kept coming, giving me cock after cock. Two more men stepped up, one at my face and another between my legs. A hot cock was slipped into my cunt, and another into my mouth.

Rubbing my stockings as he stroked me, my new fucker wormed his long snake up my canal. The fucker stroked me like a madman until he was ready to blow. I remember that he pulled it out and blasted chunks of scalding hot seed onto my cunt lips.

The man enjoying the blowjob rubbed my cum covered tits as I sucked him off. In no time he dumped his copious load of hot scum into my open, waiting mouth.

All that cock was definitely affecting me. These black bastards were driving me mad with lust. But I was getting physically exhausted from the repeated fuckings. My body could not keep up with my hormones, and my arms finally fell to the side of the table.

Oblivious to my plight, the guys decided it was time to pick up the pace. Men picked me up and placed me on the floor.

I was rolled on my side in order to give the waiting black cock free access to my cunt and ass at the same time. The first two bastards positioned their enormous black cocks at the entrance of my holes and pushed. Their hot cocks rolled into my cream-filled cunt and ass, and I could feel their big cock heads meeting in my insides.

The black studs proceeded to ream in a synchronous fucking that drove me so wild I could feel my eyes rolling in my head. When they started to long dick me in rhythm, my cock-stuffed holes convulsed by the simultaneous banging together of their giant black cock heads.

The next pair of Mandingo studs impaled me simultaneously, both black cock heads rolling inside me at the same time until they firmly lodged deep in my body.

These particular studs created such a tremendous feeling in me that I can't even begin to describe.

Eight men had me that way, on my side being double penetrated. Oh my god, how I loved to be double fucked!

The whole time, numerous other strangers would walk up to drop loads of hot scum on my head. I could feel the cum dropping on my face like it was raining.

It was a scene of wanton decadent fucking, one married white wife and mother using her delicate soft body to service a never-ending crowd of horny black cock. Covered with scum and my ass ripped raw, I couldn't move when these eight pair of studs were done DP'ing me.

I think Al was getting worried that I was going to call it a night, so he told the others that it was time to give me a rest. Al didn't realize that by that point in the night I was totally the whore, a fuck toy for any black man who wanted me. I couldn't remember who I was or that I even had a husband.

Knowing I couldn't walk, Al had two men carry me into Joe's bedroom and placed me in the middle of the bed. They removed my heels and covered me with a blanket. I quickly fell asleep.

It couldn't have been all that long when Al came in and climbed on the bed, which woke me in the process. He moved the blanket away to reveal my body. He was very gentle, rubbing his hands gently over my cum-encrusted tits and face.

It felt good, so I just closed my eyes and let him enjoy me. I didn't care when he gently climbed between my legs and slipped his black cock into me. Al stroked my well-lubbed gaping cunt easily. He soon blasted another load of nigger seed into me.

I was oblivious when Al got off and another man took his place. Black men just kept coming in, crawling between my legs and creaming my cunt. As cum would ooze out of my cunt, the next man would take his place and pish it back in with his cock. Physically exhausted, my hormones were still willingly taking one hot cock after another.

It seemed that not all of the men were men, though. As out of it as I was, I could tell that some these blacks had to be boys getting their first taste of pussy. What a first piece of ass it had to be for the lucky black boys -- a beautiful white wife and mother with a fertile cunt!

Each black man Al could find was taking full advantage of his chance to mate with me, to fertilize my womb. They were all very gentle, however, so as to not upset the apple cart. The studs just stroked their big black pricks off in my wet cunt and ass.

Soon, a towel was placed beside me so the men could wipe off the cum dripping from my cunt before the next mounted me. I had become a cum repository, a place for these fucking black men to come and empty their balls all night long.

All of the fuckers had me. Anybody who wanted me could have me. My womb had to be literally filled with their sperm. The greater danger, however, was that I subconsciously became more of a depraved slut as each cock took me that night.

As I drifted off with strange men mounting me and creaming between the legs, my mind raced from the days activities.

I couldn't believe I had done this. I was literally covered in cum and was still taking more. I reveled in it, a real cum slut as Al had diagnosed. Not caring about any repercussions, I did realize that if I did get pregnant, I would never know who the bastard was who actually implanted his baby in me.

Yes, a trip to the doctor was in order.

Chapter Fourteen

At about 5:30 a.m. I heard Al pulling the last man off from me. He shuffled the crowd of black men out of his house.

I felt thoroughly reamed, each hole searing from the brutal attacks they withstood. I was relieved to be free of cock, but it was an admission I refused to share with Al. For some sick reason, I wanted this man to know that I was the best whore he could ever dream of meeting.

Once the last man had left, Al came into the bedroom and grinned down at me.

"I knew you'd never let it stop, Andrea."

He was right.

I took on a countless number of huge, hard black cocks. Even in a half passed out state, I would voluntarily spread my legs for any man and allow him to use me to service his rod of only he'd give me cum.

I couldn't understand how in twelve hours time, I turned from an innocent, young wife into a sex starved bitch who would let all those black men gang bang me.

I fell asleep in Al's strong arms, my mind dreaming about black cocks and how many young wives this man had remade into his slut. We slept for about an hour, until early morning when Al rolled over and kissed me on the lips. The kiss woke me, and I was groggy when he ran his tongue into my still sticky mouth.

Al stopped to moan, "God, baby, you were really great."

We continued to kiss for a few minutes, by body still radiated from the afterglow of a long night of heated fucking. I couldn't believe that I fucked all of those black cocks! I never felt like such a woman before, a lusty woman born to service horny cock.

I instinctively reached down between us and grabbed for Al's black cock in my sleepy state. I took the prick in my hands and stroked it hard as we kissed. I then felt Al's hand lift my leg so he could stick his horny black cock into my sore pussy one more time.

Al only needed to take a few deep strokes before he creamed.

"Ahhhhhh, Andrea, I love your cunt," he cooed, "you can always be my slut."

When Al had finally finished with me, he asked me how I felt.

"My body's sore, but actually I feel pretty good," I informed him.

He was quick to point out the obvious. "A life of fucking agrees with you, baby."

The words were true, and this man taught me that. On hearing his words,

I wrapped my arms around his back and we started a deep kiss.

"Thank you baby," I said.

"Thank you for a wonderful night, and thank you for taking care of me."

Al just passionately kissed me.

When we stopped kissing, I glanced at the clock.

Oh, no!

I panicked at the time, I was so late for work at the bank. I thought about it for a minutes, and picked up the phone to call in sick. As sore as my pussy and ass were, sick time was clearly called for.

I was the assistant manager, so I had to talk to the manager, Jack. The asshole who yelled at me the day before and sent me home -- allowing this whole thing to get started.

When I called Jack, the bastard screamed at me, telling me I was worthless. I was too sore to care, and hung up on the rude bastard.

When Al asked me about it, he commented that a lady with my talents like me shouldn't have to put up with assholes like him. He offered to take care of the situation, but I told him it would be alright. Violence never solves anything.

I looked in the mirror and was shocked. I was covered in dried cum, and my hair was disheveled and stuck together from dried wads of sperm. Wads of caked dried cum were on the sheets between my legs. I felt like a used whore, and I loved it!

But I was exhausted. I needed to sleep.

Alone.

I showered and fixed myself up. Except for the lack of pantyhose, you couldn't tell I looked any different than I did when I went to work the day before. The stockings Al gave me were covered in dried cum, so I left them behind for Al to keep as a souvenir. Just like Bill had a souvenir!

As I was about to leave, Al took me in his strong arms. I gave him a long, deep kiss goodbye and thanked him Al asked if he could call me sometime. While I was hung over, my sensibilities were coming back. I told Al that I needed to think about it, but I agreed to take his number. I stuffed it into my purse and started to head out the door.

"Thank you for helping my son," Al said as I walked out, "I won't forget it."

I was shocked! Nickie was his son! That's what he meant when he told me not to hurt his boy?!? I couldn't believe that I deflowered Al's son!

"You're welcome, sweetheart," I calmly said in response.

Joe gave me a ride back to the bar where I had left my car, which was only a few minutes away. By now the beer had worn off, and my mind was racing with all of the events of the past 24 hours. Joe and I didn't say a word the whole trip. He just reached under my skirt and rubbed my naked thighs.

My husband was still out of town with Ginger, so I avoided explaining the lack of pantyhose. I crawled into bed and just slept until he came home that night with Ginger and woke me.

I told Mark that I stayed with my friend as I told him the night before, but that I had gotten sick in the meantime and was slow to get home. I felt guilty as hell when he believed me, bringing me dinner in bed.

So ended my first day ...

The Story Continues

The weekend had arrived, and I spent Saturday in bed as well. By Sunday I was up and enjoying the cool spring day. I went to church and thought long and hard about what had happened.

I went home and sat by our pool, unable to get the images of Thursday out of my mind. My feelings were a whirlwind of confusion, torn between the lust I had experienced and the sincere love I had for my husband.

I resolved that being a slut was not how I was raised, and that it was wrong to act that way. I didn't want to betray my husband or screw up my marriage. I decided that I would let life go on as it had before Thursday, and do my best to forget about the fuckfest of which I had been the center. I also resolved to not tell my husband because I didn't want to put that kind of burden on him.

The last resolution got a little difficult for a few days, and terror seared through my soul when I missed my period. Odds were that it was a black baby given all the black cum Al made sure was pumped into me. It would be impossible to tell my husband that it was his.

I decided to wait a few weeks to see. Sure enough, my period was late. But I didn't take any kind of pregnancy test. I couldn't live with an abortion, I thought, and it was probably best not to verify it. I quickly went to the doctor and took care of any issue with a D&C.

My mind raced constantly with the life altering questions, and my mind drifted more and more while I was at work which just pissed my boss off more. What an asshole.

I was worried that my husband would find out. Being such a trusting man, he believed me that night, which made me feel more horrible. I truly was happily married, and I told myself that I wouldn't fuck around like a whore. So, I continued with my life, pretending as best I could that nothing had changed.

The whole encounter did have its up side.

It gave me a new appreciation of how beautiful and desirable I was. While I always cared about my appearance, I now gave special attention to make sure that I looked great. I know I couldn't fuck, but I could still feel like the sexy woman that I was. I went out a bought more sexy heels, skirts, dresses and suits, most admittedly short. Nothing sluttish mind you, I just wanted to be the beautiful and sexy professional woman that I was.

I also decided to take Bill's suggestion, and I went to the store to buy a whole series of stocking and crotchless pantyhose. My body was still covered, so who cared? My husband liked them a lot, so it wasn't long before I wore them exclusively, trying always to wear a skirt or dress so I could wear them.

I also gave special attention to my jewelry, hair, and makeup, ensuring that they were always perfect. I felt beautiful, and I WAS beautiful!

The new emotions flowing through me were too much, though. The soreness had gone away, but the emotions hadn't. I had a non-stop aching between my legs that I had never had before, a feeling that demanded that I be regularly man-handled and fed hard cock. And hot cum. God, did I love the taste and feel of thick, sticky cum.

I started to miss it so much, I thought I would go crazy. I wanted so much to deep throat my husband and suck the seed from his balls, and I wanted him to fuck my ass. But I was afraid he would want to fuck me and discover how large my holes had gotten since we last had sex. Mark was getting horny, too, but out of fear, I had to push him off. The bedroom was a dreadful place for me.

I wouldn't have sex again with another man for another year. A lot happened in that year. My sex life continued to grow incredibly frustrating. I didn't want to cheat on Mark, but I didn't know how to explain to him that I've discovered that I love sucking cock, eating cum, and taking hard pricks up my ass.

Later, Mark and I decided to have another child. I thought that would help. But it didn't. And then I went back to work after a long maternity leave . . . and life changed.

It was becoming increasingly difficult to deny to myself that I had become a raving nymphomaniac within a short 24-hour period, and my strength was almost at an end.

I invite you to read about the next year of my life in *Seduced Tramp*!

Author's Perspective

A number of people have written to me to ask my thoughts on the book. I thought I would share some of my perspectives with my readers . . . well, those of you who care!

Why do I do write these books? Because I enjoy writing, and I think the stories I have to share can help people through their marriages. I find that I am a very sexual person, and these books help me to explore that aspect of my life.

The things discussed in these books are meant to entertain through fantasy and, to a degree, to give you an idea of the lives other people lead. Perhaps they can give you or your spouse ideas on spicing up your sex life.   Is it immoral? I don't think so, but I'm no expert on morality. I can tell you that I am a fairly religious person. I go to church every Sunday, and the fact that I write these books does not bother me at all. I hurt nobody, and I always try to help people. Does God care? I think not. As long as we don't hurt others.

And what about you? I suppose if you bought the book, you have an interest in the contents. There's absolutely nothing wrong with that, I think. But please remember a theme that you will see in every book I write . . . the value of family.

Whatever you do, both myself and my publisher encourage you to work at keeping your marriage and family together if the two of you really love each other and respect each other. As they say, marriage is a full time job! It would be wise to be aware of and somehow control the monster known as jealousy. Jealousy is an interesting thing. At its worst, it gives you that nauseating feeling when you feel your spouse is cheating on you. You want to know all of the details, and you are literally obsessed 24/7 with the thoughts. It is truly paralysing. Why put your spouse through those emotions? If you love them, perhaps a discussion – finding a solution you can both agree on – would be best. Or just leave. If you can't do either, you are unfortunately in a predicament that I am not qualified to judge or assist.

On the other hand, jealousy can be a good thing if it is controlled. Two major problems I have seen and experienced for years is boredom and taking someone for granted. When you know your spouse has an admirer, however, you now risk the loss of something important to you. You (hopefully) realize its importance and share your feelings with your spouse. Or perhaps some flowers and a kind word of how beautiful or handsome he/she is. But why wait for that admirer to come around? Remember – Everyday is a good day for romance. And the great sex that comes from it . . .

This all reminds me of something that I recently heard on a podcast. It was by a lady called Emily. She regularly does a 2-minute women's perspective podcast. This one dealt with threesomes. Reversing the genders of what she said, she commented that the most important rule is that, just because your partner consented to this one encounter does not mean that all rules are waived . . . even with the same person . . . even the same day! If you have sex with another man while your husband is in the room with you, that's kinky. If you do it while he's in the shower, it's cheating. Thanks Emily – you're a very insightful lady. Something for all of us to think about!

So, until next time . . . be happy, be safe!

– Jennifer

www.ingramcontent.com/pod-product-compliance
Lightning Source LLC
Chambersburg PA
CBHW020125180626
46810CB00004B/1407